The Eleventh Orphan

Joan Lingard

Catnip

In memory of my grandparents,
Maggie Sophia and Alfred Henry Lingard,
who ran a pub in Green Lanes,
Stoke Newington, in London
in the early years of the twentieth century.

CATNIP BOOKS
Published by Catnip Publishing Ltd.
14 Greville Street
London
EC1N 8SB

First published 2008
5 7 9 10 8 6 4

Text copyright © Joan Lingard

A CIP catalogue record for this book is available from the British Library.

ISBN 978-1-84647-052-3

Printed in Poland

www.catnippublishing.co.uk

The
Eleventh
Orphan

Chapter One:
The Pig and Whistle

When the eleventh orphan turned up, Ma Bigsby hesitated. She told Elfie later that she'd always said she wouldn't take in more than ten at a go. It was a nice even number and she currently had five of each. She'd felt that if she took on another one it would tip the balance.

'I'm not sure, son,' she said to Constable O'Dowd, while eyeing Elfie.

Elfie clutched her bag to her chest and shifted her bare feet about on the cold pavement. The woman was staring down at them. So they were none too clean, but she couldn't help that, could she? When you had to doss down under a bridge you didn't have much chance of cleaning yourself. It wasn't her fault either that her jumper was holey and her skirt ragged.

Ma Bigsby herself was wearing a big canvas apron wrapped around her middle, over a steel-grey dress that matched her hair. She stood in the doorway of the public house, feet planted wide apart, sleeves rolled up to the elbow, with her broad hands parked on her hips.

'What's her name?'

'Elfie.'

'Never come across that before.'

'Seems it's short for Elfrieda.'

'What age is she?'

'Eleven. So she says.'

'Small for her age then.'

Elfie glared at the woman. What a bloomin' cheek she had, calling her small! Who was she to talk? She wasn't all that tall herself, not for a grown woman, and she was almost as wide as she was high.

'How much do you know about her?' asked Ma Bigsby, continuing to speak about Elfie over the top of her head. 'Been thievin', has she? Is that how you know her?'

'She's a bit light-fingered.'

Elfie glared at him now. She'd thought the copper was her friend. He'd said he was.

'What has she took?'

'Couple of apples.'

'If that's all!' Ma shrugged.

'More or less.'

'Oh well, kids have to eat.'

'You never spoke a truer word, Ma. I'm not going to run them in for a couple of apples or bananas.'

'You're a kind-hearted copper right enough.' Ma Bigsby looked back at Elfie. 'He's let you off a few times then, has he?'

Elfie said nothing. She'd said nothing since the constable had persuaded her to come with him. It seemed that he and Ma Bigsby had known each other of old and whenever he called in at the *Pig and Whistle* she'd give him a glass of Guinness to warm him up. They both hailed from County Cork in the south of Ireland. Ma Bigsby ran a good house, he'd said. She didn't stand much nonsense but she was kind and Elfie would get a roof over her head and some hot dinners. Elfie had still not been very sure but when he'd said the pub was at the foot of Green Lanes in Stoke Newington and called the *Pig and Whistle*, she'd agreed to come.

'You're not havin' me on? That's its real name?'

As soon as they'd drawn near and seen the pub's sign hanging up ahead she'd known that this was the right one. Constable O'Dowd had been sure that it would be. He didn't know any other pubs with that name in London and it looked like the one in her picture. But then he only patrolled his own beat so he couldn't swear on it.

'I don't allow kids that live in my house to go out thievin',' said Ma Bigsby. 'I've got my standards. Pa Bigsby don't like it either.'

What would Pa Bigsby be like, wondered Elfie.

'I'm sure she'd give it up, wouldn't you, Elfie?' said Constable O'Dowd. 'I mean, there'd be no need.'

She was continuing to say nothing.

'I usually like to take them in when they're younger,' said Ma Bigsby, pursing her lips. 'Afore they're eight years old. More chance of training them in our ways.'

What ways were those? Elfie began to shuffle a few steps backwards, thinking that this might not be such a good idea after all. She'd had enough of training in the orphanage, being made to scrub floors till her knuckles bled and her knees ached from kneeling. And if you missed a bit here and there you were cuffed around the head until your ears stung. That was why she'd run away. And maybe she should run away from this and all, before it was too late.

Constable O'Dowd was nice and she liked him. He'd given her sugar buns and the odd penny when he'd come across her and he'd said that Ma Bigsby might seem a bit rough on the outside but she had a heart of gold inside. Elfie had met a few of those people before who were supposed to have golden hearts but they'd always let her down in the end. She trusted no one. Now she was not sure that she wanted to be here even if it was the right *Pig and Whistle*. Where would that get her anyway? She might be better off sleeping under her usual bridge where she knew all the kids. She wouldn't call them friends exactly but she knew where she stood with them. More than one had tried to nick her special bag. 'What have you got in there that's so precious?' they'd kept asking. She'd never told them. She had guarded the bag with her life and that had made them even more curious. Sometimes she'd have a bad dream and wake in a panic, thinking it was gone. That would be the worst thing that could happen to her.

'It'd be a nice deed to do on the first day of the new millennium, wouldn't it, Ma?' said the constable.

It was the first of January, 1900. Elfie had heard midnight strike on Big Ben. The streets had been full of people cheering.

'I suppose it would be.' Ma Bigsby was still studying Elfie from head to toe as if she were trying to make up her mind.

'There's another reason I've brung her here. Show her the picture, Elfie.'

Elfie kept the bag close to her. She hated showing it to people and usually only opened it when she found a quiet corner to herself. Then she'd take out each of the items and study them closely. She had opened it for PC O'Dowd when he'd said he'd take her to a public house called the *Pig and Whistle*.

'Go on, show her, Elfie,' he urged.

Elfie reached into the canvas bag and took out a small watercolour painting, mounted on cardboard. It was a little creased though she'd tried her best to keep it neat and clean.

'Let Ma Bigsby have a look then! She'll give it back to you, don't worry about that.'

Reluctantly Elfie handed it over.

Ma examined it at arm's length. 'Cor blimey, if it's not our *Pig and Whistle*! Says so at the foot. Where did you get that from, luv?'

'Me mum.'

'And where's your mum now?'

'She's dead.'

'Died just after Elfie was born,' said the constable. 'That's how Elfie come to be an orphan. The hospital put her in an orphanage.'

'And what had her mother to do with my pub?'

'That's what we don't know. It's a mystery.'

'In that case,' said Ma Bigsby, 'you'd better come in, child.'

And before she knew it, Elfie was inside the *Pig and Whistle*.

Chapter Two:
Ma Bigsby's Orphans

Elfie followed Ma Bigsby into the public bar. The place seemed well kept, she could see that at a glance. The light was dim since it was not yet opening time but even so the mahogany bar shone and the brasses were bright enough to blind you. Ma obviously ran a good show. Elfie had been in pubs before, when she shouldn't have been, she wasn't denying that. She'd been begging and men with a pint or two of bitter in them were often more generous than those walking the street. The smell of beer and cigar smoke was familiar to her, and the sawdust on the floor.

The chairs round the tables and the high stools at the bar stood empty at this time of day.

'Well, what do you think?' demanded Ma.

'Looks nice.' It was a sight better than some of the grubby ones she'd been in.

'I'm particular, remember that and you'll get on well

enough with me. I like everything shined up good and proper.'

'Will I have to do that?'

'Everyone has to do their bit in my house. We've all got our chores. Some of the older girls have wee jobs outside like sewing buttons on shirts, to earn a bob or two towards their keep. I don't sell enough beer to feed thirteen mouths. You any good with a needle and thread?'

'Never tried.'

'Thought not. Cleaned brasses?'

'No.' Elfie eyed the horseshoe brasses on the walls and the rail round the top of the bar and the handles of the beer taps and the knobs on the cupboards and doors. There was an awful lot of the yellow stuff.

'You've a lot to learn, girl. Are you willing?'

'Suppose so.'

'What kind of answer's that? I want a straight answer, either yes or no!'

'All right, yes, then,' muttered Elfie.

'I'm taking that as a promise. First thing is to get you up the stairs and into a bath and scrub the dirt off you.'

Elfie might have cut and run then and there if Ma hadn't bolted the big door behind them.

'Probably got nits too, have you?'

At the mention of nits, Elfie scratched her head. Who didn't have them, or fleas, come to that?

'We'll soon see to that. A drop of paraffin will do the trick.'

Pour paraffin on her head?

'And we'll chop a bit of that tangle off while we're at it.'

'I don't want my hair cut,' wailed Elfie. She didn't want to end up with hair like Ma's. Her own was curly, though, not straight, and of course it wasn't grey, but dark brown.

'It'll have to be cut or we'll never get all the beasts out of it. Don't you want to have a nice comfy head that don't itch?' Ma glanced at the big round clock ticking on the wall. 'It'll be opening time soon.'

She began to work her way around the walls, putting a match to the gas lamps, until the room was filled with warm, flickering light. Elfie smiled for the first time since arriving at the *Pig and Whistle*. The place had a magical look now. It mightn't be so bad here after all. Anyway, if she didn't like it she didn't have to stay, did she?

'Course you'll not be allowed in the bar during opening hours,' said Ma, descending, groaning about her knees. 'Right stiff they are. I was sixty last birthday, you know.'

'I could light the gas for you another time,' offered Elfie. 'I could climb up.'

'Well, we'll see how you get on.'

The swing door at the back of the bar opened and in came a young woman dressed in a long black skirt and a cream satin blouse with a frilly collar and leg-of-mutton sleeves. Her hair was swept up at the back, held by a comb, and she wore a choker of three strings of pearls round her throat and long dangly pearl earrings. Elfie drew in a breath. The woman looked beautiful.

'This is Florrie, our barmaid,' said Ma. 'She used to be one of my orphans; came here when she was five. She's in lodgings along the street now that she's a young lady. Florrie, this is a new girl. Name's Elfie.'

'Hello, Elfie.' Florrie gave her a dazzling smile.

'Hello,' said Elfie, her eyes transfixed by the earrings swinging in the light. If she stuck in here at Ma Bigsby's she might get to be a barmaid when she grew up and wear a pearl choker like Florrie's.

'We'd better get on up the stairs and see to that bath. I'll be back down to give you a hand at the bar later, Florrie.'

'Right you are, Ma,' said Florrie, moving in behind the bar to start polishing glasses.

Elfie gave her a backward look, wishing she could stay with her, and followed Ma through the swing door into the nether regions of the pub.

'Kitchen for the bar's through at the back. And the lavvy for the customers. You're not to use that. We've got our own on the floor above.'

Elfie trudged after her. Kids were making a noise overhead. Sounded like a couple were squabbling.

Ma opened the door of the parlour. 'What's goin' on then?' she demanded.

'He took my skippin' rope!'

'Did not.'

'That's enough,' said Ma. 'We don't allow rows about

stupid things like skipping ropes, you know that.'

The boy and girl confronting each other backed off. They were both tiny.

'This is Elfie, come to live with us,' declared Ma and straightaway they seemed to be surrounded by boys and girls, who were now silent, and all staring at Elfie. Ma began her introductions. 'I'll go in order of age for you.'

First came Mabel, just turned fourteen. 'She's an absolute angel with the wee ones.'

Mabel blushed. She was a big girl with a cheerful grin, freckled face and bright ginger hair. She smiled at Elfie, showing that she had two teeth missing at the front.

'And here's Joe. He's thirteen.'

Joe was black. Very black. Elfie stared at him and he stared back at her with the biggest brown eyes she had ever seen, with a look that said, 'What do you think you're staring at?' She'd only ever seen one black man before and that was a sailor down at the docks.

'He's a great reader, is Joe,' said Ma.

Next in line came Billy, aged twelve. His ears stuck out like handles at the sides of his head. He was mad about trains and wanted to be an engine driver.

Ivy, eleven, had thin, tow-coloured hair and angular bones that seemed to stick out in all directions. She screwed her face up at Elfie.

'This is where you'll fit in, Elfie,' said Ma. 'Alongside Ivy.'

Elfie didn't fancy being placed beside that one.

Nancy and Dora, seven-year-old twins, looked as alike as two peas in a pod, though Ma pointed out that Dora's mouth was wider than Nancy's. That was one way to tell them apart.

Then came the babies, four of them, all under five years old: Albert, Vicky, Sam and Cuddles. It had been Vicky and Albert who'd been fighting about the rope. Cuddles was only eighteen months old and Mabel had him up in her arms shoogling him about.

'Where she gonna sleep?' asked Ivy.

'In the girls' room, of course.'

'We only got five mattresses.'

'We'll soon find another one. Now I want you all to be very kind to Elfie and look after her until she's found her feet.'

Ivy wasn't going to look after her, Elfie felt sure about that. She'd marked her down as an enemy from the minute she'd set eyes on her.

'Put Cuddles down, Mabel,' said Ma. 'It'll do him good to crawl about a bit. It'll help strengthen his limbs. And come and help me with Elfie's bath.'

Ivy sniggered. Ma gave her a long hard look until she dropped her eyes.

They went into the kitchen, Ma, Mabel and Elfie.

'Fill the bath, Mabel, while I go and find some fresh clothes for Elfie. Ivy's should fit her.'

'I don't want to wear somebody else's clothes,' said Elfie. Especially not that girl Ivy's. She began to back away. The copper hadn't mentioned anything about baths; he'd spoken only of hot dinners and a roof over her head.

'You'll just do what you're told, madam. And when the shops open up the morrow I'll buy you some new ones. That's if you're good, mind.'

Ma left them and Mabel fetched a tin bath, which she set down in the middle of the floor. She then filled a saucepan with hot water from the tap and proceeded to pour it into the bath. Elfie watched with mounting horror.

'Best get your clothes off.' Mabel was already starting to fill another saucepan. It would take a few to get the water up to a decent level.

'*All* o' them?'

'You can't go in a bath with anything on! Better get a move on. Ma'll be expecting you to be ready when she comes back. And put your bag down. You can't take that into the bath with you, though it looks like it could do with a good wash.'

'You're not washing it!' Elfie held it close.

'I'm not going to touch it. Stick it up on the shelf where it'll be safe.'

Elfie could stall no longer. She let her skirt slide down to her ankles, then she slowly took off her jumper and stood there in a grey shift that might once have been white.

'Come on now,' said Mabel, 'off with your shift and your drawers.'

'I ain't got no drawers.'

'The shift then.'

Elfie hadn't been stark naked since she was at the orphanage, and that was a year or two back. She covered her chest with her arms.

'Hurry up,' urged Mabel.

Elfie was blowed if she was going to strip off in front of her. Quickly she picked up her skirt and jumper and pulled them back on.

'Don't be silly,' said Mabel.

'I don't want no bath,' cried Elfie and, seizing her bag, she made off down the stairs.

There must be a back way out of this place. She saw an open door and went through it into a yard stacked with beer barrels. A delivery man was about to roll one right across her path. He straightened up and stared at her.

'What you doin' here? Breakin' in, was you?'

'She's a new girl, just joined us.'

Elfie whirled round to see Ma standing in the doorway. She backed away. She wasn't joining anything.

'You can't keep me here,' she shouted. Just let them try!

'Course I can't,' said Ma. 'This isn't a gaol.'

'You're daft if you don't stay,' put in the man. 'Kids that fetch up here are the lucky ones, you can take my word for it.'

Elfie frowned.

'Come on in with me, Elfie.' Ma held out her hand. 'If you're wantin' to go let me give you some clothes for your back at least so that you don't freeze to death.'

There could be no harm in that. And it was perishing cold outside. Elfie didn't take Ma's hand but she followed her back up the stairs to the kitchen where the tin bath steamed gently.

'You know,' said Ma, 'you'd feel an awful lot better for a good soaking. You're not scared of water, are you?'

Scared?

'Course not,' scoffed Elfie. 'I ain't scared of nothing.'

'Want to try it?'

'As long as it ain't too hot.'

'We're not going to scald you.'

Elfie kept her eyes lowered while she took off her clothes. She had a few scabs on her body that she didn't like them looking at. Flea bites that had got infected after she'd scratched them.

Mabel seized her hand and held on to it until she was safely in the bath and sitting down. There was just room to sit if she drew her knees up to her chin. The warm water did feel quite good lapping round her. Nice, and sort of comforting.

'We'll do your head first,' said Ma. 'Hold this bit of towel over your face, luv, so that you don't get no paraffin in your eyes.'

Elfie covered her face and bowed her head. She howled when the stinging paraffin hit her but Ma paid no attention. She slapped on the soap and then her strong fingers began to work at her scalp, pummelling and digging, going deeper and deeper, until Elfie felt sure she must be reaching right into her brain. For a moment there was a lull but it didn't last long for Mabel was filling a big can of water for the rinsing.

'Keep your eyes shut tight, Elfie,' instructed Ma. 'Otherwise they'll sting.'

They already did.

A flood of water came cascading over Elfie's head and face and went running down into her eyes, her nose, her mouth. She wanted to howl again but she could hardly breathe.

'We'll need another jug, Mabel,' said Ma. 'Soon be over, Elfie.'

Elfie thought the second dousing would drown her.

'Right then, luv,' said Ma. 'Lift your head. I'm going to give it a good rub.'

First she wiped Elfie's face dry, then she pummelled her head with a rough white towel.

'Me head aches,' yowled Elfie.

'Sure, it'll settle down in a wee minute. Now up you get and stand in the water.'

'Can't I get out now?'

But Ma hadn't finished. She soaped Elfie's body all over with a bar of yellow carbolic soap and then Mabel got rinsing with her cans of water. Finally, Elfie was allowed to step out of the horrid tin bath on to the kitchen floor. When she looked down she saw that the water was filthy.

'There now,' said Ma, standing back to admire her handiwork, 'aren't you the nice clean girl!'

Elfie had never been so clean in her life.

But the agony wasn't over yet. After she'd been dressed in clean, new underwear and a dark-blue skirt and jersey, she had to sit with her head bowed again, but at the table this time, with a sheet of white paper in front of her. Ma took a steel comb with narrow teeth from the shelf and began to comb out Elfie's tangled curls. That was almost worse than the paraffin for her hair was full of tugs with large clumps stuck together. She wailed and screamed from the pain of it and Ma urged her to try and stomach it for the sake of getting out as many beasts as possible.

When Elfie was allowed to lift her head she saw that the paper was littered with small insects, some looking as if they'd died in the flood while a few were still crawling.

'See all that rubbish that was in your hair? You didn't want to let them keep feeding on your blood, did you?'

Elfie gaped at the nits. She didn't know that was what they'd been doing.

'It'll take a wee while to get rid of the lot. We'll douse you once a week until we do.'

Once a week! To go through all that again? Would it be worth it? Then Elfie looked back down at the insects and she said nothing.

'All the girls and boys have a weekly bath. I like a clean house and clean children.'

Elfie wondered if Ma washed herself like this once a week. The tin bath didn't look wide enough to hold her.

'The first wash is the worst,' said Mabel, trying to console her.

'Are you hungry?' asked Ma. 'Don't think I need to ask, do I?'

The last food Elfie had eaten had been in a Salvation Army soup kitchen the day before, when she'd been given half a mug of thin greasy soup and a chunk of stale bread like a doorstep. She'd gone there most days.

Ma set a bowl of steaming hot porridge in front of her, with a spoonful of rhubarb jam floating in the centre. Elfie ate fast, her elbows on the table, keeping her head down.

'We don't like elbows on the table,' clucked Ma, 'but I'll let that pass seeing as this is your first day. Fancy a bit of bread and cheese now?'

She paused. A man's voice could be heard outside on the landing.

'That'll be Pa back,' said Ma. 'He's a real gent, is Pa, so mind your manners, Elfie. He's a scholar, to boot.'

Elfie stopped eating and lifted her head. She wondered what a gentleman scholar would be like. She'd never met one before. The door opened, and in came Pa Bigsby, dressed in a three-piece lavender suit, grey top-hat, silver-grey spats over shiny black shoes, and carrying a silver-topped cane.

Chapter Three: Pa Bigsby

Pa Bigsby had a mane of white hair and twinkly blue eyes. He was not all that tall for a man but he did stand a full head higher than Ma. His wife. Elfie was trying to sort this out in her mind. The two of them didn't look as if they would belong together, he in his fancy suit, and she in her canvas apron, but they must, for here they were. Constable O'Dowd had told her that since they didn't have any children of their own they'd decided to take in orphans. They'd started with two and then another had arrived on their doorstep, and so it had gone on.

Elfie didn't have any experience of matching up husbands and wives. She didn't know if her mum and dad had matched or not. To begin with, she didn't know who either of them was. But she was bent on trying to find out. That was why she was here. She wasn't just after the hot dinners.

Pa Bigsby was beaming at her. 'So we have a new girl in the house! Florrie told me when I came through the bar.'

'Yes, this is Elfie,' said Ma. 'I've just been cleaning her up.'

'Welcome, Elfie, to the *Pig and Whistle*! You look as clean and fresh as a daisy.' He came and shook her hand. No one had ever shaken her by the hand before or said she looked like a daisy. He sat down beside her. 'Tell me, child, can you read and write?'

'Pa's the teacher in the house,' put in Ma. 'He gives lessons every day in every subject under the sun. History, geography, Latin, astronomy, botany. Religions of the world. Grammar. Oh, and arithmetic, though he's not so fond of that, are you, Pa? He's very keen on grammar, though, so you'll have to mind your p's and q's.'

Elfie had no idea what grammar was.

'I like to hear people speaking the Queen's English and speaking it correctly,' said Pa. 'No dropped aitches for a start.'

'He's very fond of ancient Greece and Rome too.' Ma spoke proudly. 'And reading and writing, of course.'

'Can't do either o' them,' muttered Elfie, ashamed at having to admit it. She knew her letters and she could recognize the names of streets and shops but that was about all. She hated the thought that she might be shown up by that Ivy girl.

'Not to worry, dear,' said Pa cheerfully. 'I shall give you some extra tuition. You look a bright girl to me. I'm sure you'll pick it up quickly.'

She wouldn't put her money on that, if she had any.

'Do the kids not go to no school then?' she asked.

'*Any* school,' said Pa.

'No need,' said Ma. 'When the man from the Education Board came round I instructed him to write "home-schooled by private tutor" on his form.'

Elfie could imagine Ma standing up to the man and him turning tail and running.

'He had the nerve to ask me if the tutor was educated! I sent him away with a flea in his ear. I told him he most certainly had been educated, in the university of life.'

'And the library,' added Pa. 'When you've finished your meal, Elfie, I'll take you upstairs to my study and we'll make a beginning.'

'*Right now?*' She was only just recovering from being half drowned.

'No time like the present, I always say.'

There seemed to be no arguing with him. Elfie got up and let him lead her up the stairs to the next landing where the children's dormitories, the schoolroom and his study were situated. He and Ma slept on the floor below, he explained, next to the parlour.

Pa Bigsby's study was a small room under the eaves, stacked with books. Elfie gawped. You could hardly walk across the floor. She had never seen so many books, except when once she'd gone into a library to get warm and been chased out.

'I don't know if I'll be any good at the learning.'

'Of course you will! You must have confidence in yourself. If you don't, you will not advance in life.'

It was all right for him to say that, in his lavender suit

and pearl tiepin and his gold watch on a chain across his chest. Must be worth a bob or two, that. One of the kids she'd run about with had found a gent's watch and they'd tried to pawn it, but the pawnbroker had called the police and they'd had to drop it and run for their lives. It wasn't as if they'd nicked it! Weren't finders supposed to be keepers? The police didn't always see it that way, mind you.

Pa taught reading by getting his pupil to recognize words printed on cards. He had a big stack of them, in different colours.

'Blue for nouns, *things*, like cat and mat and girl and boy,' he said. 'Green for verbs, the *doing* words, like walk and talk; pink for adjectives, the *describing* words, like tall and small. Don't worry about the other colours for we will get to them eventually.'

Elfie wasn't worrying about them. She had enough to bother her with blue, green and pink.

'It will all become clear in time,' Pa reassured her.

Once he was satisfied that Elfie could recognize the letters of the alphabet, he began by holding up a blue card.

'The word says CAT. I want you to look at it carefully and then say it after me.'

Elfie said it.

The next word said MAT.

'Point to which letter is different.'

She pointed, thinking she might enjoy this after all. They continued, and by the end of the session she could read, 'The hat sat on the cat and the cat sat on the mat and got fat.'

'Excellent, Elfie!' declared Pa at the end of the lesson.

She went downstairs to the parlour where the twins were colouring pictures in a book and Ivy was playing ludo with Joe and Billy.

'I can read,' announced Elfie.

'Bet you can't!' retorted Ivy.

'Bet I can!'

Ivy put down the dice shaker and grabbed a book and opened it. 'Read that, then, smarty!'

Elfie stared at the black, close-packed print, searching for any words that looked like cat, mat or hat.

'Come on, Ivy,' said Joe. 'It's *Treasure Island*. You can't read it yourself, it's too hard for you.'

Treasure Island, thought Elfie. She wouldn't mind reading that. She was going to work hard at the cards.

Ivy was glowering at her.

'Come on, throw the dice, Ivy,' said Billy.

Ivy tossed it on to the board and they resumed their game. Elfie sat in a chair by the window and looked at the coloured pictures in the book. *Just let Ivy wait!* She'd show her!

The pub was open down below. They could hear men's voices and some laughter and then came a snatch of song. Elfie listened. *There's an old mill by the stream, Nelly Dean* . . . She'd heard that before. An old drunk down by the bridges used to sing it. He'd gone on so long one night that a dosser had shouted out, 'Why don't you go and drown yourself in it?'

After a supper of bread and dripping and a cup of milk, Mabel chased them up the stairs. She'd already got the little ones to bed. Elfie needed no chasing. She was bone-tired. It had been a day like none other and she hadn't got much sleep the night before. It had been cold and damp under the bridge and somebody had nicked her best blanket, leaving her only a scrap of a thin one. Her newspapers had been damp too.

She settled down on her pallet, placing her bag beside her head, where she could reach out and grab it should somebody try to do a snatch.

'What you got in that scabby old bag?' asked Ivy. 'The queen's jewels?'

'None of your business. And it ain't scabby.'

Elfie was on the verge of sleep, about to go under, when she sensed someone moving near her. She pushed her hand out from under the blanket and groped about on the floor. Her bag wasn't there.

She shot bolt upright and yelled, '*Thief!* Somebody's nicked me bag.'

There was commotion in the room and Vicky started to cry. Mabel lit a candle. Elfie carried on yelling. She knew full well who would have taken her bag.

Ivy slung it back across the room at her. 'Take yer silly old bag. It stinks.'

The door opened, and in came Pa Bigsby. 'What's going on here, girls?'

'She stole my bag!' Elfie pointed to Ivy.

'I didn't steal it. I were just goin' to take a look at it.

24

What's she got in it, that she wants to hide? Bet it's stuff she's stole.'

'*Stolen*,' said Pa. 'You had no right to take someone else's possession, Ivy, you know that very well. Nor to accuse anyone wrongly. Apologize to Elfie.' When Ivy hesitated he added, 'Or you will not qualify for the special treat of the month.'

'Sorry,' muttered Ivy, but she wasn't, Elfie knew that. As well as being a thief, she was a liar.

'Perhaps I should take the bag up to my study, Elfie,' suggested Pa, 'and keep it safe overnight?'

'Oh no, I never let it leave me.' Elfie clasped it against her body, covering it with both arms.

'You can trust me, you know,' he said gently.

She hesitated before saying, 'Well, all right. But you'll not go lookin' in it, will you?'

'I give you my word that I will not.'

He lifted the bag, said, 'Good night, girls. Sleep tight, sweet dreams!' and left the room.

Elfie scrambled after him, catching him up in the doorway of his study.

'Are you still worried, dear? You don't have to be.'

'It's just that I got very special things in there that belonged to me mum.'

'I understand.'

'Some of them might be about me dad.' Elfie hesitated. 'I was thinkin', with you bein' a scholar, maybe you could help me read them?'

'I'd be delighted to, Elfie.'

Chapter Four: Elfie's Bag

Thirteen round the table was something of a squash. Ma Bigsby told them cheerfully to keep their elbows in.

'No diggin' your neighbour in the ribs now!'

'If it weren't for *her*,' began Ivy, pointing at Elfie.

'That'll do, Ivy,' said Ma. 'And you know it's rude to point.'

Cuddles sat at the end on a high chair banging a spoon on the tray. Everyone was chattering, making quite a din, everyone except Elfie, that was. She'd felt in a daze ever since she'd woken up that morning to find four strange girls lying on mattresses alongside her.

Pa banged on the table with his spoon and called for quiet so that Ma could say Grace. They bowed their heads and Elfie noticed that some children closed their eyes, and some did not.

'For what we are about to receive, may the Lord make us truly thankful,' recited Ma. 'Amen.'

Heads lifted, eyes opened. Thinking that must be the signal to start eating Elfie stretched out her hand and seized a piece of bread. If you weren't quick you mightn't get anything, she didn't have to be told that.

'She grabbed,' cried Ivy and then, turning to Elfie, said in a prim voice, 'We ain't allowed to grab.'

'*Aren't*,' said Pa. 'Elfie is not yet used to our customs. It will take her time to learn them. When we are offered something, Elfie, and we take it, we should always say thank you.'

Elfie dumped the slice of bread back on to the plate, folded her arms across her chest and glowered. She didn't want their stupid old bread. They could stuff it up their jumpers.

'You didn't have to put it back,' said Pa, holding out the plate. 'Please do have some bread.'

She hesitated. She'd like to say no but she was hungry. Keeping her eyes lowered, she took a piece.

'Now what do you say?'

'Ta.'

'Another time "thank you" would be better,' said Pa gently.

'You'll soon learn,' said Joe in an aside to Elfie. He seemed a quiet boy. She had noticed that he had his head stuck inside a book half the time.

She said nothing for the rest of the meal. It seemed to go on for ever. No one was allowed to leave the table until everybody had finished eating and had eaten everything on their plate. Waste was not tolerated in this house, Ma informed Elfie, who hadn't cleared her porridge bowl. There were an awful lot of rules to remember and Elfie didn't like rules. She wasn't used to them and was wondering all over again if she'd be able to stick it here. Then she thought of the cold under the bridges and her bag and the hope that Pa Bigsby might be able to help her track down her father. Once she had she'd be able to leave the *Pig and Whistle* and go and live with him.

Ma had her eye on her. Elfie scraped up the last spoonful of cold porridge.

Finally Albert, who had been taking his time, shoved his last crust into his mouth.

'You may now leave the table,' said Ma. 'But, first, what d'you say?'

'Thank you for a nice meal,' chanted the children, after which there was a stampede and a great scraping of chairs as the children made off. Only Ma and the two on dishwashing duty remained. The children had to take turns for various chores, the boys as well as the girls. Elfie was about to leave when Pa called her back.

She turned. Perhaps he was going to give her her marching orders, tell her he didn't want someone who grabbed food living in his house.

'I was wondering if you'd like to tell me about your bag? We have a little time before classes begin.'

Elfie nodded.

'Let's go up to my study then.'

Passing Ivy on the landing she stuck her tongue out at her, behind Pa's back.

Elfie liked his cosy little room, especially when he closed the door and shut all the others out. Her bag lay on his desk. She picked it up.

'You value it greatly, don't you?'

'It was me mum's. It's got her keepsakes in it. I think some of them could be about me dad. I'm hopin' they'll help me find him.'

'I believe you don't know his name?'

Elfie shook her head. 'I don't know me mum's either.'

'*My* mum's,' said Pa. 'That does make finding people difficult. Well, let us see if we can find any clues in your bag.'

Before delving into it Elfie glanced round to make sure that the door was properly shut and no Peeping Tom was trying to snoop.

First she took out the watercolour of the *Pig and Whistle*.

'Now why would your mother have had a painting of our public house?' mused Pa. 'Do you know anything at all about her?'

'I never see'd her.'

'*Saw*,' said Pa. 'There must be some reason she had it in her possession. What else do you have?'

Elfie dropped a gold locket into the palm of his hand.

'Aha!' Pa clicked it open to reveal a sepia-coloured photograph of a man. The man was staring straight at the camera, looking severe. But then that was how people usually looked in photographs, they had to sit still for so long.

'That could be my pa,' suggested Elfie.

'It is certainly a possibility.' Pa spoke cautiously. 'But not a certainty. It could have been your mother's brother or father.'

'I think it's him,' said Elfie stubbornly.

Pa Bigsby was examining the photograph closely, with the help of an eyeglass. 'It's not a very clear picture but it would appear that the man is young and has darkish hair. Beyond that, one cannot say.'

He laid the locket down beside the painting.

The next item to emerge from the bag was a gold signet ring.

'Let us see if there are initials on it.' Pa lifted the eyeglass again. 'There are! A.T. And it is a man's signet ring.'

'How d'you know?'

'Signet rings are usually worn by men. And this one would be too big for a lady's small finger.' He slid his own into it. 'It's quite loose on me so the man who wore it must have been bigger and broader than I am.'

Elfie had imagined that her father would be. In her dreams she saw him as tall, dark and very handsome.

'We are making a little progress,' said Pa. 'What now?'

Elfie produced a piece of tattered white paper on which were written two names: Alfred and Elfrieda.

'I think this explains why they named you Elfrieda at

the hospital. From this I would deduce that your mother wished to call you Elfrieda if you were a girl, and Alfred if you were a boy.'

'After me dad?'

'*My* dad. Alfred does begin with an A.' Pa lifted the ring again.

'So he could have been called Alfred?'

'He could.'

'What can the T letter be for?'

'Oh, all manner of surnames. Alfred Timpson. Alfred Tennyson. Have you heard of Alfred Tennyson? Alfred *Lord* Tennyson? The poet?' Pa began to quote. '*On either side the river lie, Long fields of barley and of rye.* They are the opening lines of his great poem "The Lady of Shalott".'

'He might have been my pa!' Elfie was excited.

'I think not, child. He died in 1892.'

'What other names start with T?'

'Numerous ones. Taylor, Trimble, Thackeray, Thomas, Templeton.' Pa rhymed them off. 'I could go on for a long time. We can hardly search the whole of London for a man called Alfred T.'

'No,' agreed Elfie gloomily. 'London's too big. It'd take ages.'

'For ever! Besides, we do not even know if he lives or has lived in London.'

'He must have when he met me mum.' Pa looked at her and she mumbled, 'My mum.' This could give you a headache, really it could.

'Very good, Elfie. Your father might have been visiting. From any part of the United Kingdom. Ireland, Scotland, Wales. Or the Isles of Man or Wight.'

The door opened, making Elfie jump and cover up her bag. But the intruder was only Ma who had come to tell her husband that it was time for the children's lessons. She had a look at the objects on the desk.

'My da's called Alfred T,' Elfie told her.

'We *think* he may be,' said Pa. 'Elfie means the initial T, by the way, not the tea which comes from India or Ceylon. One of my ancestors was a tea-planter in India, Elfie. Do you know where that is?'

She shook her head.

'We shall have to have a lesson with the globe.'

Elfie was not sure what a globe was but did not say.

'His ancestors lived all over the world,' said Ma.

'Not me, Elfie,' said Pa. 'I grew up in Stoke Newington.'

'He was brought up in a big house at the north end of the borough,' Ma went on.

'Your dad must have had a few bob,' said Elfie.

'A few.' Pa smiled.

'He had gold mines in South Africa,' added Ma.

'My father had one mine,' said Pa, 'but unfortunately it did not yield much gold. He was inclined to make bad investments. He'd get carried away by an idea. In the end he lost all his money.'

'What a shame!' cried Elfie.

'I took after my father. I proved not to be much good with money myself.'

'Were you homeless?' Elfie couldn't imagine him sleeping rough, especially in that suit, though she'd known one or two gents down on their luck who had.

'Almost. I was living in one room. My parents had sadly died.'

'He caught pneumonia real bad,' Ma carried on. 'He was at death's door. Collapsed in the street, he did, on the pavement, right outside the *Pig*.'

Pa took up the story again. 'Ma brought me in and nursed me back to life and by the time I regained my strength I realized that I could not live without her.'

They both laughed. Ma's eyes streamed and she had to wipe them dry.

'Best put your things away now, Elfie,' she said when she'd recovered. 'They're getting restless down there.'

They could hear them.

Before putting the locket into the bag Elfie showed Ma the photograph. 'Would you ever have seen him?'

Ma pursed her lips, then shook her head. 'Afraid not, luv.'

'Will I ever find him?' cried Elfie. 'I been lookin' for the man in the locket for years. Everywhere I go I looks.'

'*Look*,' said Pa. 'We might find him if we persevere, child. We have only just begun.'

'He's a perseverer, is Pa,' said his wife.

'My motto, Elfie, is *Nil obstet*.'

'That's Latin,' explained Ma.

'The language of ancient Rome,' added Pa. 'We shall

be studying Everyday Life in Ancient Rome. A most fascinating subject. As, of course, is Greek mythology.'

Elfie's head was beginning to spin.

'*Nil obstet* means that we shall let nothing stand in our way.'

'I think I'll 'ave that for my motto too,' said Elfie. '*Nil obstet*,' she repeated.

'Bravo! I might make a Latin scholar of you yet, Elfie,' said Pa Bigsby, rising from his chair.

Chapter Five:
Pa Bigsby's Class

The first lesson of the morning was poetry. Pa Bigsby read 'The Lady of Shalott' to them, all of it. The twins were fidgeting before he finished and Ivy yawned in the middle but Elfie was engrossed by the story of the beautiful lady who could spin a magic web with colours gay and the bold, red-cross knight Sir Lancelot, who rode on his war horse down to Camelot singing *Tirra lirra* by the river. She could imagine her dad charging on a fine horse down to the river.

'What did you think of that then?' asked Pa as he closed the book.

'I liked it.' Elfie spoke up without thinking. 'It was awful sad though that the lady had to die because of a curse. I wished she hadn't.'

She couldn't help feeling sad herself now for she was wondering if her mum had had a curse put on her.

'I don't believe curses like that happen in real life,'

said Pa, as if he'd read her mind. And maybe he had! 'Only in stories and poems.'

'I heard old Molloy cussing the other day,' said Ivy. 'He was shouting his 'ead off at a boy who'd bin trying to nick an apple off 'is stall. You could 'ear 'im 'ollerin' all the way up the street.'

'Aitches, Ivy, aitches!' Pa shook his head.

'I don't suppose the boy dropped dead,' said Joe.

Ivy looked annoyed. 'How do you know? He might 'ave died when 'e got round the corner.'

'Unlikely, Ivy,' said Pa. 'And I don't like to hear you saying "Old Molloy". You should refer to him as *Mr* Molloy.'

'Everybody calls 'im that,' she muttered.

'We are not everybody,' said Pa. 'We are *us*. We have better manners.'

So far, so good, Elfie was thinking. If all the lessons were like this, listening to Pa talking and reading poetry, she'd be able to manage fine. But the next one was writing. That was different. She could write her name, well, sort of, but that was all. Reading was another thing she couldn't do much either.

Pa was giving out writing books. They were lined, and on the top line of each page were words that even Elfie could see were beautifully written, with the letters all slanting the same way, and lovely loops and curls. They were to copy them on the blank lines below. They were sitting in a row at a long bench and she had Ivy on one side, and Joe on the other. They had books with big words. She had smaller ones, the same as seven-year-old Dora and Nancy. Ivy gave her a smug look. She was going to have to wallop her before she was done, thought Elfie. Good and hard.

'Fill the inkwells, please, Joe,' said Pa. 'And, Ivy, would you mind giving out the pens?' He himself handed out pencils with soft leads, and a rubber, to Elfie and the twins.

'Now don't worry, Elfie,' said Pa. 'Just do your best and if you're not pleased with a word just rub it out and try again.'

She did so much rubbing that she almost made holes in the page. She sat back scowling, not liking what she saw. When she glanced sideways she was dismayed to see that Ivy's page was filled with beautiful slanting writing and no ink blots anywhere. Joe's writing was good too but not as good as Ivy's. Billy, on the other side of him, had several blots on his page and his fingers were stained with ink up to the second knuckle. This was going to take a long time to learn to do properly, Elfie could see that.

'Perseverance, remember, child,' said Pa Bigsby.

Writing was followed by arithmetic. Elfie knew her numbers and could count on her fingers but Pa did not approve of that. They must count in their heads but to help he brought out a counting frame called an abacus which had ten rows of beads and ten beads in each row. Elfie enjoyed pushing the beads along, as did Nancy and Dora.

'It's for babies,' whispered Ivy.

'Shut your gob,' said Elfie.

She saw Joe smile. What did he think was so funny? Everyone was annoying her at the moment.

By the time they stopped for lunch, a bowl of a delicious meaty mutton broth with bread and dripping, served up in the kitchen, she felt exhausted. Her head was buzzing as if it were full of bees.

She was about to lean across the table and help herself to a slice of bread when she saw Ma watching her.

'There's plenty for everyone, luv,' said Ma.

Elfie had forgotten. Well, how could she remember so many rules all at once?

Ivy gave Elfie one of her smirks and said, 'Please may I 'ave a piece of bread and drippin', Ma Bigsby?'

She was asking for more than bread and dripping, thought Elfie. A clip round the earhole, more likely.

When they were clearing up afterwards, Joe said to her in his serious voice, 'You should pay no attention to Ivy. It's just her way.'

'I don't like that way.'

'If she sees you're bothered it'll only make her worse.'

He sounded very wise but Elfie didn't feel wise herself. She felt mad.

Joe retreated to the parlour to read *Treasure Island*. He said he was going to move on to *Kidnapped* next, by the same man, Robert Louis Stevenson. That sounded good to Elfie too. But when would she ever be able to read anything as hard as that? Who could go on reading about fat cats with hats sitting on mats for ever?

In the afternoon, there was work to do, for some, at any rate. The babies were put down for a nap alongside Ma Bigsby, who herself needed to get her feet up and shut her eyes. She went to bed late and rose early. The twins were settled in the parlour with colouring books. The two older boys were employed by local businesses, running messages and delivering groceries, while Mabel, Ivy and Elfie set off for the wash-house with the washing loaded up in an old pram.

Pa Bigsby was going to the library.

'I wish I could go to the library,' grumbled Ivy, as they pushed open the laundry door and were met by a blast of hot steam. 'This is an 'orrible place.'

Elfie wished she could go to the library too, even if she couldn't read. She could always look at the pictures and it'd be nice and quiet. The steam stung their eyes while they boiled up the whites in big copper drums and soon their hair was plastered to their scalps. Elfie wiped her forehead with the back of her hand but that was damp too.

Mabel worked away at the scrubbing board, trying to clean stains from towels and tea cloths, her powerful forearms pumping rhythmically. No wonder her arms were so strong. Elfie wondered if hers would ever be like that. She supposed they might if she were forced to spend enough time in this horrible wash-house. She would far rather be out and about in the streets with the boys doing deliveries. She'd taken against the place the minute she'd set foot in it. She hated the heat and the steam and the smell of bleach and the noise of boiling and churning and rubbing and the red-faced women shouting to each other across the room. When it came to using the big heavy mangle to squeeze the water out of the sheets she and Ivy had to team up to get enough energy to push the handle right round. It was hard work and Ivy kept shouting at her to push harder. Elfie made a face at her. It was a pity Ivy didn't catch her finger in the mangle.

Emerging into the cold street after two hours, with the pram piled high with damp, clean washing, Elfie was glad of the fresh air. She didn't even mind that it had started to rain. Mabel did. She was worried the washing would get soaked through.

'Run,' she told them, setting off herself, steering the laden pram in zigzag fashion along the pavement. One of its wheels looked wobbly.

Ivy began to run too but Elfie didn't bother. She sauntered along, looking in shop windows and down alleyways to see if anybody she knew would be hanging about, not that she expected that there would be. Nor would she be all that keen to see them. This was not the patch that her old mates – if she could call them that – worked. They'd be closer to the river.

Some small kids were playing on the pavement with a spinning top and quarrelling over whose turn it was. A window opened overhead and a woman yelled down to them. Her voice was drowned out by a brewer's dray rattling past. It might be on its way with a new stock of beer for the *Pig and Whistle* though there were loads of other pubs around.

A horse bus went by, packed to the gunnels on both decks. Elfie longed to sit on the open top deck of one of those buses but she'd never come across a driver who would give her a free ride. She'd got thrown off a couple of times when she'd tried it on. Following behind the bus was a rag-and-bone cart, the poor old horse looking clapped out and ready for the knacker's yard. And then came a motor car. It was only once in a while that you saw one. Elfie stopped and gaped. The driver was wearing big leather gloves up to the elbow and no goggles. She loved it when he leant out and squeezed the big bulbous horn. That sent the rag-and-bone cart skittering into the side to make way. Until then he'd been taking up the middle of the road.

A little further along, she came upon Joe sitting on a step in a doorway, hugging his knees up to his chest.

'What you doin' there?' she asked.

'Just sheltering.'

'I'm soaking wet.'

'I like watching the rain.' He had such big dark-brown eyes. Eyes that noticed everything, it seemed, and looked sad at times.

'Want to sit down?'

'Might as well.' She didn't want to go back inside, not yet.

He shifted over and she sat down beside him and together they watched and listened to the rain drumming on the pavement.

'I like the sound it makes too,' she said.

He nodded.

When it began to ease off a little, she asked, 'You like learnin', don't you?'

'Yes. Why, don't you?'

'I don't think I'm any good at it. I can't do nothing.'

'*Anything*,' he said, and then grinned. 'Sorry! It's a habit.'

'That you got from Pa Bigsby?'

'Must have. But the lessons will get easier, you know. Took me weeks to get used to everything. And I missed my mum.'

'You knowed her then?'

'*Knew* her,' he said. 'I was five when she died. My dad died the year before her. I've got a picture of them both. Want to see it?'

'If you like.'

He took a photograph from his inside pocket and Elfie leant over to take a look. Two black people, a man and a woman were sitting side by side holding hands. They had smiley eyes, like his.

'They look nice,' she said.

'They'd just got married,' said Joe. 'They were living in Trinidad. That's in the West Indies – I'll show you on the globe. I can remember the way the flowers smelt at night-time.' For a moment he drifted away from her, then he came back. 'My dad had a good job. He was manager of a sugar plantation.'

'What did they come to London for then?'

'He must have thought it was a good idea.'

'But it weren't?'

'*Wasn't.*' Joe shrugged. 'He couldn't find a job and then he got ill.' His voice tailed off and he stared back out at the rain.

'I never knew one nor t'other of my parents.' Elfie went on to tell Joe about her bag. She didn't usually talk about it to anyone and hadn't until she'd met Pa Bigsby, but Joe had shared his story with her so she thought she could share hers with him.

'It sounds rather like a treasure hunt. Except that you've got all the clues in one bag.'

'You won't tell anyone else, will you?' Elfie asked anxiously. 'Especially not Ivy.'

He promised that he would tell no one, no one at all.

The rain had stopped, and it was beginning to darken. Afternoons closed in early in January. The lighting man, shouldering his ladder, was making his way along the street igniting the gas lamps.

'We'd best get back,' said Joe. 'Ma'll worry if we're not back before dark.'

'You like living in the *Pig and Whistle*, don't you?'

'It's my home,' he said.

She wondered if it would ever be hers.

Chapter Six: A Place Called Penetanguishene

As they neared the *Pig and Whistle* they saw Pa Bigsby standing outside, sheltering from the last drips of rain under a big black umbrella. He was sharing his cover with a man in a long grey coat who had a flat grey cap pulled down low over his eyes. When they got closer Elfie saw that he had droopy moustaches. The pouches under his eyes drooped too.

'That's Sad Sid,' said Joe. 'He'll be waiting for the bar to open. He comes every night to meet his friend Frankie.'

'He looks as if somebody has just stole his toffee apple,' said Elfie.

'*Stolen*,' said Joe.

'What's he sad about?'

'Ma says it's his nature. He lives with his sister Mad Meg, though she's not supposed to be really mad, just a little dippy in the head. He misses the Emerald Isle. He's

Irish, you see, like Ma. And half the other folk round about.'

Elfie wondered if everyone had got something to be sad about. Ma and Pa Bigsby didn't seem to. They were cheerful all the time. Ma was always singing in the kitchen, songs about Ireland mostly. *The Rose of Tralee* and *The Mountains of Mourne* were two of her favourites.

Pa had spied them. 'You youngsters are late out.'

'We been watching the rain,' said Elfie.

Both Pa and Joe let that slip of grammar pass.

'Haven't seen you before, miss,' said Sad Sid, eyeing Elfie.

'She is the latest addition to our family,' explained Pa.

'Don't know how you do it.' Sad Sid shook his head. 'Taking all those kids in off the streets.'

'We like them, Sid,' said Pa. 'That's why we do it. Come on then now, you two, inside with you, or you'll be in trouble with Ma, and you wouldn't want that, would you? You will have to wait five more minutes, I'm afraid, Sid. Ma is very particular about not opening up until it's time.'

'Don't I know it!' he said mournfully.

Pa furled his umbrella and, opening the door, ushered the children inside. He then bolted it, leaving Sad Sid to shelter as best he could outside.

Florrie was behind the bar polishing glasses. Her earrings were whirling.

'Hello, you two! What have you been up to then?'

'I were at the wash-house,' said Elfie, drifting over to the bar to get a closer look at the earrings.

'*Was*,' said Pa.

Florrie smiled. 'He'll not let you off.'

Elfie already knew that.

After supper she found she was on dishwashing with Billy while Joe and Ivy were the driers. It took four to get all the evening dishes done. Elfie felt she'd had enough of sinks and hot water that day but there was nothing else for it but to roll up her sleeves and get on with it. Ma ignored her moans and groans.

'Take your time now, Elfie. You're making an awful clatter and slopping water all over the floor.'

The next moment there was a crash as a dinner plate slipped through Elfie's soapy hands.

'Lord love us!' cried Ma. 'Me good plate.'

'It weren't my fault,' wailed Elfie.

'She's always saying that,' said Ivy.

'Oh well, never mind, it's only a plate,' said Ma. 'It's not as if it's an arm or a leg.'

By the time the dishes were finished Elfie's front was soaking.

'I bought you some new clothes the day,' said Ma. 'Spent nearly all me money!' How was it that Ma got to make mistakes in her grammar and not be checked by Pa? When Elfie asked Joe afterwards, he said that was because she was Irish. They had different ways of speaking. In the West Indies they also said some things differently. And it could be that Ma had been too set in her way of speaking by the time she'd met Pa.

Elfie was excited, however, at the thought of the new clothes. Who wouldn't be!

'I got you some underwear and a nice dark-blue dress for every day,' Ma went on, 'and a red velvet one with a lace collar for Sundays, and a navy serge coat to keep you warm. I'll show you them after.'

Elfie loved the dresses, particularly the Sunday one. She would wear red velvet when she went to meet her father. She was hoping that Pa would call her up to his study in the morning.

But he didn't, and she was disappointed. He must start lessons sharp, he said, as he had business to attend to in the City that afternoon. He was away till suppertime.

'Sorting out our finances,' said Ma. 'Such as they are.'

Florrie told Elfie, when she went down to have a chat with her in the bar, that Ma and Pa lived hand-to-mouth. 'No wonder, with so many mouths to feed. Though Ma's good at making the money stretch. She knows where to get bargains.'

It was the same the following day. Pa was gone from noon till six o'clock in the evening.

On the third day, he said to Elfie, 'I think we might snatch half an hour this morning.'

After breakfast Elfie raced up the stairs to the top landing, passing Ivy on the way.

'Where you goin'?'

'None of your business,' said Elfie.

As she made to go up the next step Ivy stuck her foot out, sending Elfie sprawling. But not for long. In a flash she was up and back on her feet and after Ivy. She caught her by the hair and pulled hard. Ivy screamed and turned to lash out at Elfie. The din brought Pa Bigsby from his study. The girls fell back.

'Now, now, what is going on here? I hope you've not been fighting?'

'She pulled my hair,' cried Ivy. 'She near tore it out at the roots.'

'She tripped me up,' yelled Elfie. 'She started it.'

'You both know we do not allow fighting in our house. It is one of our rules.'

'Wait till I get her outside,' thought Elfie. 'I'll thump her good and proper.'

'I want you to say sorry to each other.'

'I ain't sayin' sorry to 'er,' said Ivy.

'I ain't either,' said Elfie.

'Very well. Then perhaps neither of you will be on the next treat. I was thinking we might go to Buckingham Palace to see the *Changing of the Guard*.'

Both girls were thinking. After a moment, Ivy mumbled, 'Sorry', but Elfie knew she was lying. Pa was looking at her now.

'Sorry,' she muttered and, in a low voice that reached only Ivy, added, 'Like 'ell I am!'

'Off you go then, Ivy. And remember, peace be on this house!'

Ivy went down the stairs. Elfie carried on up and followed Pa into his study. He told her to pull up a stool beside him at the desk and handed her the bag.

Taking care she lifted out an old newspaper cutting. It was yellowed with age and some of the print had faded. Pa peered at it through his eyeglass.

'It's to do with a sailing from Southampton to Halifax, Nova Scotia, but the date and the name of the ship are missing, unfortunately for us.'

'Where are they, them places?'

'*Those* places. I'll show you on the globe.'

Elfie had never seen one before. This was the world, Pa told her, spinning it in front of her eyes.

'The world?' she echoed. 'But it's round like a ball.'

'And that is just what the world is.'

'How can it be? It are flat, I can see it are flat!'

'*Is*,' said Pa. 'It is only an illusion. The world *is* actually round, Elfie. You have to take my word for it. Scientists have proved it.'

'What are all them blue bits?'

'Seas and oceans.'

'But there's an awful lot of them.'

'There is more water than land in the world.'

'Honest?'

'Yes, honestly. I would not lie to you, Elfie.'

'And the pink bits?'

'Those are countries that are part of the British Empire.'

She was finding out so many new things that she

wondered if her head would have space for them all. It might burst first.

'Now, here,' said Pa, twirling the world around on its stand and bringing it to a halt with his finger, 'is Southampton, on the south coast of England, where the ship was to sail from.' He spun the globe some more. 'We are crossing the Atlantic Ocean now and here is Canada, a much bigger country than ours. It would take several days to get there by ship. It may be that Alfred T made that trip. But we need another clue.'

'I've got a letter.'

'That sounds promising.'

'Part of one, anyway. It got tore off at the bottom.'

'*Torn*,' said Pa.

Elfie handed it to him.

'It is headed "Georgian Bay House, Penetanguishene",' he announced, taking his time to pronounce each syllable. 'Pen-etang-wisheen.'

'Funny name, innit?'

'*Isn't it*? Only to us because it is not familiar.'

'Where is it?'

'I'm afraid I do not know, Elfie. I have to confess that I have never heard of it.'

A place that Pa Bigsby had not heard of!

'Maybe it don't exist?'

'*Doesn't*. No, it must. It is an interesting name. It might very well be in Canada and, if so, that would tie in with the boat ticket.'

'Can't you find it on that round ball?'

'If it's a small place it wouldn't be there.' He took a quick look and shook his head. 'Only the major cities are marked.'

'Can you read it to me?' Once or twice Elfie had thought of asking someone to do it but had shied away from the idea, for you never knew whom you could trust or what the letter might say.

'I can indeed,' said Pa Bigsby.

The letter read as follows:

My dearest,

I arrived here on the 12th after a somewhat lengthy journey due to exceedingly inclement weather. Canada is a vast country, as I am finding out. I travelled here from Toronto by the Grand Trunk Railway, which in fine weather I daresay functions perfectly. We had lengthy delays due to heavy late snowfalls.

Tomorrow I start work. I have much to learn, which I hope will be of use to me when I come back to London in two years' time. It seems such a long time to be away from you!

Yesterday, walking down Main Street, I came across Nettleton's Jewellery Store, which enjoys a good reputation in the town. On impulse I went in and on seeing this locket—

The rest of the letter was missing.

'The locket!' cried Elfie, pulling it out of the bag. 'He must have sent it to me mum! My mum,' she added, making Pa's eyes twinkle.

'It seems a reasonable conclusion,' he agreed.

'Imagine, he weren't going to come back for two whole years!'

'*Wasn't*. It would have been a long time for someone to wait. And sadly . . .' Pa did not go on for they knew the rest. Elfie's mother had died before then. 'The letter is dated 8 July 1888. When were you born, Elfie? Do you know?'

'Course. It was all written down at the orphanage. It were the first of February 1888.'

'*Was*,' said Pa. He looked thoughtful. 'It is possible then that this man *is* your father.'

'There's another piece of paper in the bag that's got that big long name on it as well.' Elfie rummaged and found it.

'It's an advertisement for the hotel,' said Pa.

Georgian Bay House
Penetanguishene

This house is well known and needs no
commendation, while special care and
attention will be devoted to anticipate
and supply the desires and wants of the
travelling public. Terms moderate. Free bus
from all trains and boats.

Best brands of Liquors and Cigars

Good Sheds and Stables
and Attentive Hostlers.

CHAS. DEVLIN,
Proprietor

'I shall have to give this some thought and do a little research in the library. Leave it with me, Elfie.'

Ma came in to see how they were getting on. Pa gave her the letter but before reading it she had a word with Elfie about fighting.

'But it weren't my fault,' wailed Elfie.

'*Wasn't*,' said Pa.

'I never said it was,' said Ma. 'But the two of you have to cut it out. I've spoken to Ivy.'

'I 'ate her,' muttered Elfie.

'That is not the right spirit, Elfie,' said Pa. 'You must learn to love each other.'

'*Love?*' said Elfie.

Ma turned her attention to the letter. 'He has a good hand and he writes well, doesn't he now?'

'He is obviously an educated man,' said Pa. 'And here is the hotel where he was lodging.'

Ma studied the leaflet. 'Sounds like a nice establishment. Wouldn't be cheap, not like a working man's hostel.'

'My pa might be rich,' said Elfie.

'Pigs might fly,' said Ma.

'Or blow whistles,' added Pa with a smile.

'Nuisance, though,' said Ma, 'that he didn't put her name at the top instead of writing "My dearest". That doesn't give you much of a clue, does it?'

'He wasn't to know we'd be looking for clues,' retorted Elfie hotly.

'All right, keep your hair on! I was only passing a remark. You do have a quick temper on you at times, girl, don't you?'

Elfie glowered.

'But he must have been in love with your mum,' Ma continued. 'At least that's nice for you to know.'

Chapter Seven: Weekend at the Pig and Whistle

There were no lessons on Saturday, which was good news for Elfie. Her head needed a rest, but when she saw Joe sitting with his nose in a book she wished she could read too. He seemed to be enjoying himself and sometimes he smiled and his eyes lit up. Even Ivy was reading. Her book had coloured pictures. When Elfie sneaked a look she saw a heap of fairies in different-coloured dresses flitting about in the air. She'd rather have a story about treasure or dragons.

Billy was studying a comic and the twins were playing *Snakes and Ladders*. Mabel was up in the schoolroom with the little ones singing *Ring-a-Ring o' Roses*.

Elfie wandered into the kitchen.

'You got nothing to do?' asked Ma. 'You can come shopping with me.'

Elfie put on her new serge coat.

'Pleased with it, are you?' asked Ma.

'It's lovely.'

'Button it up now and pull the hood up too. Remember always to keep your head and your feet warm. That way, you keep the heat in.'

Ma herself was wearing a big loose black cloak that flapped about her as she walked. It made her look even wider.

They took the old pram to carry the shopping in on the way back. Ma had to buy everything in large quantities.

The streets were busy, both in the road, and on the pavements. Elfie steered the pram in between the pedestrians, doing her best not to run into the backs of their legs, having almost clipped one and been cautioned by Ma.

'Don't be letting the pram run away wid you now!'

They went to the butcher's where Ma purchased a side of beef.

'We always have a good dripping roast of a Sunday,' she said, 'with Yorkshire puddin' on the side. It's our special treat. Rest of the week it's cheap cuts.'

Elfie had never been inside a butcher's before. She'd never been tempted for there would be nothing you'd want to nick there. You couldn't imagine running off with a lump of raw meat! She eyed the carcasses hanging from the ceiling on their hooks and kept well clear of them. One was still dripping spots of blood on to the sawdust on the floor. There was a steady thump, thump, as the butchers in their blue-and-white-striped, bloodstained aprons wielded their cleavers on the cutting blocks. Elfie decided she didn't much care for the sight and smell of so much blood.

The butchers knew Ma.

'Still feeding the five thousand, are you, Mrs Bigsby?'

'I'm not the only one in these parts with a big family.'

'You're right, missus. Mrs Moon up the street has fourteen.'

Next was the baker's where they bought five large loaves and then on to the greengrocers to load up with vegetables.

Outside there they bumped into Constable O'Dowd.

'Top of the morning to you!' said Ma.

'And the same to you two ladies! Settling in all right, Elfie?'

'She's like one of the family,' said Ma. 'Will you be popping into the *Pig* the night, Kieron?'

'I might, at that.'

'He's sweet on Florrie,' said Ma, as she and Elfie set off again.

'Is she sweet on him and all?'

'Florrie's biding her time.' Ma smiled. 'She has a few suitors.'

Elfie hoped Florrie would pick the constable. He'd been nice to her and once when she'd nicked an orange he'd let her off. Perhaps she should put a word in for him to Florrie.

'They'll all be in the night, like as not,' said Ma. 'We always have a good singsong on a Saturday night.'

After they'd been to the ironmonger's, the chemist's, the candlestick maker's and, finally, the grocer's, where they loaded up with heavy bags of sugar, flour and tea and slabs of butter, lard and cheese, the pram was piled high and beginning to sag on its wheels. Ma had to give Elfie a hand to push it now.

'It's carried a few babbies too, this pram, in its time,' she said. 'It's earned its keep.'

They made one more stop, at the confectioner's, where Ma bought a big bag of toffees and one of striped black-and-white balls.

'It's not good for their teeth, I know,' she said, as she handed over the money. 'But once a week it'll not do much harm.' She confessed to being rather fond of striped balls herself.

'Sure, doesn't everyone need a little treat now and then?' said Mr Merriweather.

'My thinking exactly,' said Ma, stowing the bags in the pram.

They were almost home when suddenly the pram gave a lurch, and the back wheel, which had already been wobbling, went twirling across the pavement into the road. The whole thing collapsed, almost taking Ma and Elfie with it. Potatoes, cabbages, oranges and turnips went rolling across the pavement into the gutter, bags of flour burst, a bottle of bleach bought at the ironmonger's broke. Elfie grabbed the bags of sweets.

'Oh my Lord!' cried Ma.

To add to the confusion, the loose wheel of the pram had struck a pennyfarthing and knocked its rider off, a long thin man wearing checked knickerbockers. The cycle lay on its side, its big wheel spinning like mad. The man was scrambling to his feet and shouting his head off.

'I might have been killed!'

Behind him a brewer's dray had had to come to a quick halt. The driver was none too pleased either. One of his beer barrels had rolled off the back and he had plenty to say about that. And, at the back of him, a horse bus had been forced to brake, jerking the passengers forward in their seats. That driver was out in the street too, making a noise.

Passers-by were stopping.

'Elfie, run and get Joe and Billy!' ordered Ma who, for once, sounded flustered. 'Tell them to bring the wheelbarrow from the yard and a brush and shovel.'

Elfie ran, dodging in and out of the crowd, and entered the *Pig and Whistle* by the back door.

'Help!' she cried. 'We've knocked a man off his bike and there's one 'ell of a mess in the street.'

'You did *what*?' asked Pa, peering down from the top landing.

'The pram wheel come loose.'

Joe and Billy dropped what they were doing and came hurtling down the stairs. They ran, trundling the wheelbarrow in front of them. Pa followed, walking briskly, with Ivy bringing up the rear.

The shouting and arguing in the street had not abated. A policeman, who had happened on the scene, was trying to calm everyone down. The cyclist was claiming his machine was ruined. The brewery driver was swearing he'd sprained his wrist getting the stray barrel back on board.

'Perhaps I can help sort this out, Constable,' said Pa.

His arrival in his lavender suit, top-hat and silver-topped cane had had a quietening effect. There was something about his voice too, thought Elfie, that made everyone stand still and listen.

'May I examine the cycle in question?' he requested.

The man brought the pennyfarthing over.

'An admirable machine,' declared Pa, making both the large and the small wheels rotate. 'Seems to be working perfectly smoothly.'

'There's a scrape on the paint,' said the cyclist sullenly.

'Ah, yes, I believe there is. A small one. Would a shilling help towards its repair?'

Pa put his hand into his trouser pocket and produced the coin. The cyclist took it and made off.

'Lucky to get it,' said Ma.

'Well, I don't know about that, dear,' said Pa. 'After all, he did take a fall.'

The brewery driver, after taking a good look at Pa, decided that his wrist was recovering.

Meanwhile, the boys had been scooping up vegetables and recovering loaves of bread and somewhat bashed bags of flour, tea and sugar. When all that could be rescued was in the wheelbarrow there was still a considerable mess left on the pavement. Ivy and Elfie were ordered to fetch buckets of soap and water and clean it up.

'As quick as you can now!' said Ma. 'And no yowlin', Ivy!'

'We don't want anyone slipping and breaking their legs on it,' said the constable.

'That would be most unfortunate,' agreed Pa.

'It were nothing to do with me,' grumbled Ivy, as she and Elfie went to do what they were told.

'It weren't my fault, either, that the pram wheel come off,' snapped Elfie.

Ivy didn't look as if she believed her.

On Saturday nights the children were allowed to come as far as the doorway of the public bar and squat on the floor. As the evening progressed they moved further and further in. Ma was too busy to notice and by that time, anyway, the place was packed out.

Everyone was in a good mood. The fire roared up the chimney, the lamps glowed, the brasses gleamed, and Florrie's pink satin blouse shone under the lights. Two men leant on the bar in front of her, watching her every movement. Suitors, thought Elfie. One had a long pointed chin and a laugh like a donkey braying, the other was wearing a horrible black and white checked suit. Florrie would be a fool to take either of them instead of

Constable O'Dowd, or Dowdy, as the kids called him. Not that he was *dowdy*. He had golden-red hair and a fresh complexion.

This was the one night of the week that Pa Bigsby came into the bar and chatted to the customers. Joe said they'd consult Pa about some problem or other and he'd offer his advice.

Some of the men had brought their wives, it being Saturday night. The women wore their best dresses and some sported pearl chokers like Florrie's, though none could match hers, in Elfie's opinion.

Sad Sid's friend Frankie was seated at the harmonium playing popular tunes. After the customers had had a drink or two they started to sing. Ma led the way with *The Rose of Tralee*.

The pale moon was shining above the green mountain . . .

Ma seemed to be singing it right from her heart, thought Elfie, as if she really wanted to go to the green mountain. She had a faraway look in her eyes. She could have been thinking about her home in Ireland. When Ma finished the song she brightened up again.

In the middle of the evening Sad Sid's sister Mad Meg arrived. This caused a bit of a disturbance but only for a minute while he tried to get her to go home until Ma intervened and said, 'Let her be. Why shouldn't she join in the fun?'

Mad Meg sang off-key and rather loudly but no one paid any attention. Quite a few of the customers couldn't sing in tune anyway.

And then, at last, when Elfie had almost given up hope, Dowdy arrived. He was on duty and, therefore, in uniform. He placed his helmet on the bar and stood in front of Florrie. The other two men grudgingly gave way to the law. It must be useful to be a copper at times. Pity they didn't have policewomen. Elfie wouldn't mind being one and getting the chance to chase robbers through the streets. It would be more exciting than serving in a shop or sewing buttons on shirts.

On Sunday mornings they all went to church. Ma, having put the side of beef in the oven along with two trays of potatoes to roast, set off for the chapel, taking with her Dora and Nancy, who'd been born Roman Catholics, like herself. Pa took the rest to different churches each Sunday. Last week they'd visited the Methodists, and the week before, the Quakers. Today they were going to the Salvation Army Hall. The children were pleased.

'It's good fun,' said Billy. 'I like the bassoons.'

Elfie was familiar with the Salvation Army people in their navy-blue and red uniforms from visiting their soup kitchens. They ran a hostel for the homeless too. Pa said they did a lot of good work for the poor. They didn't approve of people drinking but they came into the *Pig and Whistle*, and the customers gave them money to help them with their work.

Elfie was wearing her red velvet dress with its lace collar. She loved it. She couldn't stop stroking the velvet.

She had never had anything so nice in her life before, ever. At breakfast she'd been very careful not to spill a single drop of porridge on it.

Pa Bigsby led the way along the street, stepping out with his silver-topped cane. Mabel pushed Cuddles in the pram, one with four, safe wheels, while Sam sat on the end. Vicky and Albert walked and when they flagged Billy and Joe gave them piggy-backs. This left Elfie and Ivy walking more or less together though they managed to keep a good strip of pavement clear between them. Before they came out Pa had given them a little talk about loving thy neighbour as thyself, especially on a Sunday.

A number of the Salvation Army people recognized Elfie and gave her a warm welcome. They'd been wondering where she'd got to and were glad she'd found a good home.

The musicians tuned up and the singing began. *Stand up, stand up for Jesus* . . . Elfie, who wasn't used to so much singing, thought she might have a sore throat by the time the weekend was over. They had a jolly time and Pa dropped a florin into the collecting box.

Going home, whom should they meet but Florrie and Dowdy! Elfie didn't recognize him for a minute, for he was dressed in an ordinary suit and a trilby hat. Florrie was wearing a royal-blue coat with fur round the collar and a hat to match. She was holding his arm. The children whooped, and the couple blushed.

'Good day to you both,' said Pa, lifting his top-hat, always the gentleman.

'Good day, Pa,' said Dowdy, tipping his trilby.

Florrie smiled.

The couple passed on by.

And then, without any further delay, it was home for roast beef, roast potatoes and Yorkshire pudding. The smell made Elfie's mouth water the moment she was inside the door.

Elfie decided she liked weekends, as she drifted off to sleep that night. Monday morning, dropped aitches, and the shirt factory would have to take care of themselves.

Chapter Eight:
The Shirt Factory

'Happy Henrietta and horrible Humphrey have a hungry hippopotamus in their high house,' wrote Pa Bigsby on the blackboard.

Ivy giggled. 'That's silly. You couldn't have no 'ippo in a 'ouse. It'd be too big to get in the door.'

'Repeat the sentence after me, Ivy, and remember not to drop your aitches,' said Pa, and he spoke the words aloud, saying each one slowly and carefully.

''appy 'enrietta and 'orrible 'umphrey 'ave a 'ungry 'ippopotamus in their 'igh 'ouse,' chanted Ivy, looking along the row at the rest of the pupils and grinning.

'Thinks she's smart,' thought Elfie. 'She's done that deliberately.'

But Pa persevered with Ivy until she said it properly.

By the time they'd finished with grammar they were all sick of happy Henrietta and horrible Humphrey and glad even to move on to reading, writing and arithmetic.

The essentials, Pa called them, without which you could not lead a good life. They preferred history, geography, zoology, poetry and Everyday Life in Ancient Rome.

Today, after the essentials, it was geography. The Seas and Oceans of the World. Pa wrote it on the board. Elfie was still trying to get used to the idea that there was more water in the world than land. She wondered how someone had worked it out. It couldn't have been easy.

She'd never seen the sea. Pa had promised, come summer, that he and Ma would take them for a treat to the seaside, to Southend-on-Sea, where they could paddle in the water and eat whelks. The only big stretch of water Elfie had ever seen was the River Thames; and the part she knew was pretty scummy. Sometimes dead cats could be seen floating in it. People, too, now and then. Corpses. You wouldn't fancy paddling in water like that. You'd come out stinking, if you didn't drown first. She'd heard the river was nice further down where it left the town behind and flowed through meadows and villages with thatched-roof cottages, like you saw in pictures. One day she'd go on a trip down the river. When she found her dad. He would take her. He might have a boat of his own.

'Are you listening, Elfie?' asked Pa. 'You looked miles away.'

'Away in the 'ead,' said Ivy with one of her sniggers.

'That will do, Ivy!' For once, Pa sounded almost cross.

'It were only a joke,' said Ivy.

'*Was*,' said Pa. 'And it is not the kind of joke I approve of.'

Once he'd turned back to the blackboard, Elfie stuck her tongue out at Ivy.

When they were packing up at the end of morning school, Pa motioned to Elfie. 'I intend to go to the library this afternoon.'

'And find out about that place?'

'Penetanguishene?' He nodded.

She went downstairs repeating the word in her head, doing the best she could to pronounce it.

After lunch it was time to go to the shirt factory and sew on buttons. They were short-handed and had sent word to Ma Bigsby to ask if any of her orphans could help out. They'd get paid, depending on how many buttons they managed to sew on. It wouldn't be much, no matter how fast you worked, but every little helped, said Ma. Elfie knew she wouldn't be fast.

'I don't know how to sew,' she said, hoping Ma might let her go with the boys instead.

'Mabel'll teach you. Every girl's got to learn to sew. What are you going to do when your buttons fall off?'

The best thing about the afternoon was the walk to and from the factory. Ivy grumbled the whole way, saying her legs were tired after the first half-mile, but Elfie enjoyed the chance to be out in the street again. Something was always going on. Today they saw a horse come loose from its shafts and bolt, leaving the cart it had been pulling to tip over and dump its load of manure on the road.

Once they got to the factory, it was not so much fun. In the stuffy, low-ceilinged sewing room six girls were already sitting at a long table. They seemed to know what they were doing. Their fingers, the middle ones dressed in silver thimbles, were working busily. High piles of starchy shirts lay on the table with boxes of buttons.

Miss Primpton, the supervisor, was a grim woman with steely eyes. She marched up and down behind the girls, rapping them on the shoulder with her thimble if they sewed a button on slightly askew. Elfie had seen the likes of her before, in the orphanage. The minute she set eyes on her she wanted to cut and run. But then she thought of Ma Bigsby, who would not be one bit pleased if she did. She might not get to go on the special monthly treat. Pa wouldn't tell them what it was to be next time. It was a secret. He never told them beforehand, Joe said.

'I haven't seen you before, girl, have I?' asked Miss Primpton.

Elfie shook her head.

'Have you any experience?'

Elfie shook her head again.

'I'm not surprised.' Miss Primpton pursed her lips. 'Well, we'd better get started.'

The first hurdle was to get the thread through the eye of the needle and then, once Elfie had got the hang of that, which took some doing, she faced trying to aim the point at the spots marked on the cloth.

'Are you blind or something?' demanded Miss Primpton. 'Can't you see where the mark is?'

Elfie kept her eyes down. She knew, without looking, that Ivy would be smirking. She had already sewn on six buttons. As for Mabel, her fingers, even though they were big and broad, seemed to be flying along.

When Elfie did succeed in putting the needle into the right spot, it shot right through and stabbed her in the finger, not the one shielded with a thimble, but another one. Blood spurted. Elfie cried out, stuck her finger in her mouth and sucked it hard.

'Look what you've done! You've got blood on the shirt!' Miss Primpton was by now properly exasperated. 'I am not sure that you are going to be any value to me, girl.'

Elfie looked up hopefully. Maybe she'd tell her to scram, but Mabel intervened.

'I'll help her, Miss Primpton. I'm sure she'll be able to do it. She's a clever girl.'

'I don't want clever girls. I want able girls!'

Miss Primpton whipped away the shirt to clean the blood off it.

'Just take it easy, Elfie,' said Mabel. 'Look, let me show you the way to hold your hand.'

Elfie tried, for Mabel's sake, not for Miss Primpton's, or even her own. She laboured on, stabbing herself in the finger until it felt like a pin cushion, getting the thread in a tangle and having to take out half the buttons and do them again because they were not in a straight line. She also shed blood on a few more shirts but when it was just a small bit she was able to clean it with spit.

'You seem to be all thumbs, girl!' said Miss Primpton, who rapped her on the shoulder every time she passed. Later, she was to find she had a bruise there.

Then one of Elfie's buttons, in the middle of being sewn on, somehow or other went out of control and flew across the table. Unfortunately for Elfie it hit one of the girls on the other side, smack in the eye. She screamed and clapped her hand over the injured eye.

'I hope you've not blinded her,' said Ivy to Elfie, who was worried herself that she might have done, but after a minute she was relieved to see the girl opening the eye and giving her a murderous look.

Miss Primpton said to Elfie, 'I think you are a total liability.'

Elfie was not sure what 'liability' meant but she was sure it could be nothing good.

They sweated away for five hours, until their fingers ached and their eyes were red and sore from peering through the flickering gas light. Mabel said afterwards that some of the girls worked a twelve-hour day with only a short time off for lunch and tea, often reluctantly given. The only chance of a break was to go to the lavatory though even that was questioned.

'That's the third time you've asked,' said Miss Primpton.

'I can't help it,' said Elfie. 'I've got a weakness. I don't want to wet the floor.'

'I wouldn't put it past you. You'd better go but be quick!'

The water closet was out the back and it stank. Elfie didn't need to use it. She didn't really have a weakness. She held her nose and slid past, round the corner into the street, where she stood for a couple of minutes watching some kids who were skipping and singing as their feet sailed over the rope.

There came a girl from France, there came a girl from Spain . . .

Elfie's feet tapped. She longed to join them.

She heard someone exclaiming behind her and whirled round to face Miss Primpton.

'What do you think you're doing out here?' In her rage, the woman was spitting. Elfie took a step back to keep her head out of range. 'I thought you were taking a long time.'

'I was feelin' sick.' Elfie clutched her stomach and doubled over. 'I had to come out for air. I feart I were goin' to vomit.' She felt she might well do so if she had to sew on many more of those dreadful buttons.

Miss Primpton sniffed. 'I shall request that Mistress Bigsby does not send you back again.'

Elfie managed not to smile.

She trailed back inside behind the woman.

At the end of the afternoon, by which time their eyes were aching, their shoulders were sore and their fingers were stinging, Ivy had earned nine pence, and Mabel tenpence ha'penny. Elfie was rewarded with a penny farthing.

'Is that all?' She gazed at the coins in her hand.

'Lucky to get anything!' snapped Miss Primpton. 'I'll see you tomorrow then, Mabel. And Ivy too. I've got plenty of work for you both.' She looked pointedly at Elfie to let her know that she was not included. 'I could, in fact, employ you girls for a full day.'

'Twelve hours?' Ivy sounded aghast at the idea and for once Elfie didn't blame her.

'Indeed,' replied Miss Primpton. 'That is what most of my girls do. They are not afraid of hard work.'

'And just look at their red eyes,' thought Elfie. You'd think they'd had salt rubbed in them.

'Mr Bigsby insists we have lessons in the mornings,' said Mabel.

'What use are lessons for girls like you? They just put ideas into your heads. Far better off to spend your time sewing. Ask Mrs Bigsby, if you will, to consider my request.'

When Miss Primpton turned away, Elfie stuck her tongue out at her.

'That's rude, Elfie,' chided Mabel.

'I ain't doin' no twelve hours,' said Ivy.

'Don't worry,' said Mabel. 'Ma wouldn't let you. Come on then! It's time we went home.'

With the rewards of their labour in their pockets, they set off through the dark streets to walk the two miles home. Elfie groused at getting only a penny farthing. She was sure she'd done more buttons than that. Miss Primpton had cheated her.

'It ain't fair.'

'Ma won't 'alf be mad at you,' said Ivy.

Elfie gave her a shove and Ivy shoved back. Mabel had to step between them and take hold of their shoulders.

'Just stop this, the two of you! Ma'll be *real* mad if I tell her you've been fighting.'

She walked in the middle, gripping each firmly by the hand. Neither had the energy to resist. Elfie took her mind off Ivy by wondering if Pa would have found out about that place with the big name that she couldn't quite remember.

They were all three dead tired and starving by the time they saw the lights of the *Pig and Whistle* coming up. The front door was open and a spill of yellow light shone on to the pavement. The bar was busy. Florrie's pearl earrings were in full swing.

Sad Sid, who'd been talking to her, turned to greet the girls. 'What you been up to the day then, the three of youse?'

Elfie made a face. 'Sewing buttons on shirts for a horrible old witch. I 'ated it.'

'*Hated*,' said Pa, coming into the bar. 'I fear we may have to have yet another elocution lesson, on the dropping of aitches.'

'Not more about horrible Humphrey,' groaned Elfie, making sure not to drop the aitch. She thought the word aitch sounded pretty horrible itself. She moved closer to Pa and lowered her voice so that Ivy wouldn't hear. 'Did you find anything in the library?'

He nodded.

Elfie grinned and raised her thumb. She'd known she could rely on Pa Bigsby.

'Come up to my study after supper,' he said.

'So how did you get on, luv?' asked Ma. She was behind the bar with Florrie and had her sleeves rolled up to the elbow.

'She were no good at it,' said Ivy.

'*Was*,' said Pa.

'Miss Primpton don't want her back,' added Ivy.

'*Doesn't*,' said Pa.

Ma sighed and set a pint of stout on the bar counter for Sad Sid. He seemed to cheer up momentarily when the froth met his lips.

'I don't want to go back,' said Elfie. 'My fingers are sore from where the needles stabbed them.' She splayed them out on the bar counter and Sad Sid tutted. 'I could do delivering with the boys.'

'You need strong arms for that,' said Ma, closing her fist and flexing her arm muscles. 'Some of the stuff weighs a ton.'

'My arms are strong.' Elfie tried to copy Ma, which, of course, made Ivy snigger, and then Elfie told her to shut her mouth or she'd do it for her.

'Now, Elfie!' said Pa. 'That is a very vulgar way to express yourself.'

'Yer arms need a bit of fleshin' out,' said Sad Sid, eyeing Elfie.

'They're skinny,' said Ivy.

'Look who's talkin'!' Elfie parked her hands on her

hips, the way Ma sometimes did, and faced up to Ivy.

'Give over!' demanded Ma, who was beginning to lose patience. 'I've had enough of your scrapping! On you go up the stairs and get your supper. There's a pot of good ould Irish stew on the stove. The rest of us have eaten. But any more nonsense from the two of you and it'll be straight to bed.'

Mabel and Ivy went ahead. Elfie turned back to Ma Bigsby.

'Can I go with the boys tomorrow? *Please*, Ma!'

'You never give up, do you?'

'*Nil obstet*,' she said.

That made Pa smile.

Chapter Nine:
Pa Writes a Letter

When Elfie opened the door to Pa's study she saw that a large book with coloured pages was sitting open on the desk alongside her bag.

'This is an atlas, Elfie,' Pa told her. 'It shows the countries of the world in more detail than the globe. I have resolved to buy one for my library. It is remiss of me not to have had one before.'

'You can't have every book in the world.'

'I should like to, but, no, it is not possible.'

Elfie slid on to the stool beside Pa's chair.

'Our place is in Canada, as I suspected it might be. Do you see these five big lakes?' Pa pointed to them on the map. 'This one is called Lake Huron, after the Huron Indian tribe.' He let his finger travel round along the coastline. 'Here is Georgian Bay. And there is Penetanguishene! Apparently the name means "the place of the rolling white sands".'

'I wouldn't mind going to a place like that.'

'We must now try to deduce why Alfred T did go.' Pa lifted a library book and laid it on top of the atlas. 'I have found out that Penetanguishene is a centre for the lumber trade. The wood industry,' he added.

'Wood,' repeated Elfie, frowning. 'There's a little wooden boat in my bag.'

She rummaged and brought out a small carved wooden canoe.

'It could have come from that place, couldn't it?'

'Indeed. It has occurred to me that Alfred may have gone out there to learn about the lumber industry.'

'Could you find out?'

'I intend to write to the proprietor of the hotel, Mr Charles Devlin. It is a long shot, since Alfred, if he remained in Canada for only two years, would have left in 1890. That is ten years ago, after all.'

Pa took a block of white paper from the desk drawer and, after some thought, plunged the nib of his pen deep into the inkwell and began to write. As he did so, he read the words aloud so that Elfie could follow. She sat up close to him, watching the nib move steadily and surely over the thick white paper. She was amazed that Pa could write so neatly without lines to keep him straight.

This is what he wrote:

Pig and Whistle
Green Lanes
Stoke Newington
London

2 January 1900

Mr Charles Devlin
Proprietor
Georgian Bay House
Penetanguishene
Ontario
Canada
North America

Dear Sir,

I write with a request, which you may find rather odd, but I would be greatly indebted to you if you could be of help and furnish me with any information about the matter below.

I am trying to trace the whereabouts of a young man who travelled from London to Canada and lodged in your establishment in the year 1888. The problem is that I do not know his full identity, only that his first name is Alfred, and his surname begins with the letter T.

He is most likely tall in stature, with hair on the dark side rather than fair.

*It would be too complicated for me to enter into
any explanation in this letter so I pray that you will
accept that I write only with good intent.
I am, Sir, yours most faithfully*

*Algernon Bertrand Bigsby
Proprietor, Pig and Whistle*

'You're awful good at writing letters, Pa,' said Elfie
admiringly.

'*Awfully*,' he said as the door opened and Ma came
in.

He gave her the letter.

'Mr Devlin is going to find this kind of strange,'
she commented, when she had read it. 'I mean to say,
with you not even knowing the name of the man you're
looking for!'

'Life is often strange, I have found,' said Pa. 'Which
tends to make it more interesting.'

He pressed a sheet of blotting paper carefully on
to his letter and when he was sure the ink was dry
he folded the page very neatly and slid it into an
envelope.

He then stamped the back flap with the *Pig and
Whistle* red wax seal. The only thing left to do now was
to address it to Mr Charles Devlin in Penetanguishene.

'There!' he said, sitting back in his chair.

'I hope he writes back soon,' said Elfie.

'It will take weeks to arrive, I'm afraid, child, and

weeks for his answer – that is if he does reply – to come back.'

'Weeks,' echoed Elfie. 'I don't want to wait weeks.'

Pa pointed out that the letter would have to cross the Atlantic Ocean in a ship and then go overland by train, just as Alfred T had done, to reach Penetanguishene on the shores of Lake Huron.

'And so we must have patience.'

Elfie knew she wasn't very patient. But that was how she was so she couldn't help it, could she? She had a feeling that if she asked Pa Bigsby he'd say she'd have to learn to be.

'I keep wondering how Elfie's mother came to have that painting of the *Pig*,' said Ma.

'Could she have been one of our orphans?' said Pa. 'One of our early ones.'

'Most of our old girls and boys keep in touch.'

'A few don't, though. If they move away. Or, sad to think, some might have died, and we have not heard.'

'Like my mum,' said Elfie.

'Exactly.'

'Have you anything else in the bag that would help, luv?' asked Ma.

Elfie brought out a ticket for a dance hall and a card decorated with roses and violets round the edge, with the verse *Roses are Red, Violets are Blue* printed in fancy letters in the middle.

Ma picked up the ticket. '*Happy Land Ballroom*,' she read. '*Admission sixpence.* Never heard of it.'

'Shall I read the card for you, Elfie?' asked Pa.

'Please!'

'Roses are red,
Violets are blue,
Sugar is sweet,
And so are you.'

At the foot of the card were the initials A.T. written in ink.

'He was obviously a romantic man,' observed Ma.

Elfie delved into the bag again and brought out a thistle-shaped brooch with a purple stone in the centre and an object wrapped in several layers of grubby tissue paper.

'That's my most precious thing of all.'

She slowly undid the layers of paper to reveal a gold brooch set with small stones.

'What a beauty,' said Ma, picking it up. 'I've seen a brooch like this before. One of my customers showed it to me. She'd been given it by her fiancé. Do you see how it's set with seven tiny gems?' She pointed to each in turn. 'Diamond, emerald, amethyst, ruby, emerald, sapphire, topaz! If you take the first letter of each one—'

'They spell out D - E - A - R - E - S -T,' concluded Pa. 'Dearest!'

'It's a lovely thing for a man to give a woman.' Ma sounded wistful.

'One of these days, Ma, perhaps I shall buy one for you!' said Pa. 'When I come into some money.'

'The moon'll turn blue first.'

They laughed.

'Kids have tried to nick it off me a couple of times,' said Elfie. She'd given one boy a black eye, fighting him off.

'I am not surprised,' said Pa. 'It must be worth a fair bit. I think I'd better put it away somewhere safe for you.'

'Proves the gentleman we're looking for did have money.' Ma held the brooch up to the lamp so that the jewels shone.

'Why don't you hold on to the *Roses are Red* card, Elfie?' said Pa. 'I'm sure you could manage to read it for yourself.'

'I'll take the dance hall ticket too. I'm going to ask Florrie if she knows where the place is.'

She raced down the two flights of stairs to the bar. Monday nights were quiet. The only two customers were Sad Sid and his friend Frankie, who were sitting in a corner playing dominoes. Florrie was polishing glasses, as she always was when nothing else was going on. After she'd done each glass she'd hold it up to the light to make sure there were no smears.

'Florrie,' said Elfie, 'have you ever been to the *Happy Land Ballroom*?' She laid the ticket on the counter.

'I don't ever get the chance to go dancing. I'm working every night, you see, and Sundays, well, there's no dancing to go to.'

'What a shame!' cried Elfie.

'You've got to earn a living, haven't you?' Florrie laid another glass back on the rack. 'And I like working here. Ma and Pa are good to me.' She picked up the admission ticket. 'What are you wanting to know for?'

Elfie told her.

'I'll ask Pam, who's in the same digs as me. She goes dancing most Saturday nights. What else have you got?'

Elfie showed her the card.

'I've seen cards like that before. They're quite common.'

Elfie sighed.

Ma stuck her head into the bar. 'That's where you are! Come on, Elfie, up the stairs with you, at the double. It's bedtime!'

'Better go,' advised Florrie. 'I'll let you know what Pam says.'

Elfie left the dance hall ticket with her and kept the card.

She met Joe coming out of the kitchen.

'I hear you're going to be doing deliveries with Billy and me tomorrow,' he said with a grin.

She grinned back.

When she lay in bed that night, thinking about everything they'd gone over, she and Ma and Pa, she felt she was getting closer and closer to her father. She now knew he was called Alfred, that he was kind and romantic and had sailed across the ocean to North America and had bought her mother a locket and a ring that spelled *Dearest*. She had a picture of him in her head now.

But, alongside him, her mother was still a blank. If only she had a picture of the two of them together, like Joe had of his parents.

Chapter Ten: Roses are Red, Violets are Blue

While they were still at breakfast they heard somebody banging on the pub door down below.

'Who in the name that can that be at this time of the morn?' said Ma, who was trying to insert another spoonful of porridge into Cuddles's unwilling mouth. The banging continued. 'Not very patient, anyway, whoever it is.'

Mabel went down to see and came back to announce, 'It's the man from the Education Board for you, Pa.'

Pa rose at once and went downstairs, closing the kitchen door behind him.

'Holy smoke,' said Ma. 'I hope he's not come for an inspection. If he has, you'd better all be on your best behaviour! Pa's not wanting to get a bad report. If he does you might have to go to ordinary school and you wouldn't like that!'

'They beat you if can't do your sums,' said Ivy, looking

at Elfie. 'And you don't get to do nice things like Everyday Life in Ancient Rome.'

It was one of their favourite topics.

Ma gave up on Cuddles and lifted him out of his high chair.

Pa Bigsby returned.

'Children, we have a visit this morning from a Mr Ramsbottom. He wishes to inspect our progress.'

'I've warned them,' said Ma.

'Just do your best and we will have nothing to fear,' said Pa. 'Now go and wash your hands and comb your hair and then make your way in orderly fashion to the schoolroom.'

'You'd better not let us down,' Ivy warned Elfie, as they were combing their hair, and slid away before Elfie could retaliate.

Normally there would be a buzz of talk and laughter until Pa arrived. Today they were quiet.

As soon as he came in with the inspector, Elfie felt her heart take a dive. A man looking just like this one, in a greenish-black frockcoat and spotted spats, had come to the orphanage from time to time to pick fault with anything he could find.

'Boys and girls,' said Pa Bigsby, 'this is Mr Ramsbottom. Please stand and say "Good morning" to him.'

'Good morning, Mr Ramsbottom,' they chanted.

'Good morning, children,' he replied, stroking his goatee beard, which he was to do throughout the inspection, something that made Elfie wonder if he had nits in it. She'd had her hair done again on Saturday night, after which Ma had said she hoped that would knock them all off for good.

The inspector carried on. 'We shall commence with Recitation. Who would like to go first and recite a verse for me?'

Nobody made a move so Elfie felt that perhaps she should volunteer. She had a poem ready to pop out of her head. She stuck her hand up.

'Stand,' instructed Mr Ramsbottom.

Elfie stood up and recited at speed:

'*Roses are Red*
Violets are blue
Sugar is sweet
And so are you.'

Ivy tittered.

Elfie was aware from the silence that followed that she'd done something wrong but she didn't know exactly what. *Roses are Red was* a verse, wasn't it, and she was sure she'd rhymed it off correctly?

Mr Ramsbottom, whose forehead had become creased right up to his bald head, said, 'That is not exactly what I had in mind. Something more scholarly was what I was looking for.' He swung round and stabbed a finger at Joe. 'You, boy!'

'I bet 'e thinks Joe won't know nothing,' thought Elfie. But would he get a shock!

He did. Joe got to his feet and recited in perfect tones all three verses of 'Drake's Drum'.

'Drake he's in his hammock an' a thousand mile away,
(Capten, art thou sleepin' there below?)
Slung atween the round shot in Nombre Dios Bay,
An' dreamin' arl the time o' Plymouth Hoe . . .'

He carried on.

Elfie felt she could listen to Joe reciting all day; he had a rich, treacly sort of voice.

When he had finished, Mr Ramsbottom nodded. He might have said, 'Well done!' What a right meanie! You could see it in his face. A nasty bit of work. Elfie knew his type.

'Do you know who wrote the poem?' asked Mr Ramsbottom.

'Henry Newbolt,' said Joe.

'You may sit.'

That was the end of Recitation. They moved on to an inspection of their writing books and sums' jotters. Elfie considered asking to go to the lavatory but Ma had said there was to be no asking out. They were to go beforehand.

The inspector moved along the bench, stroking his beard, nodding every now and then, making little comments. When he reached Elfie he stopped and bent over her writing book. She was worried she might gag but knew she'd better not. That could put the tin lid on their chances. The man's frockcoat smelt as if it had come out of a rag-and-bone shop and he had filthy fingernails to go with it. Once upon a time she wouldn't have noticed that, but now she did. Ma was forever asking them to show her their nails.

'What age are you, girl?' asked the inspector.

'Eleven.'

He straightened himself up and addressed himself to Pa Bigsby. 'This writing is disgraceful for a girl of her age.'

'Elfie came to us just ten days ago. Before that she had not been to school. I consider that she has made good progress during her short time here and will learn quickly.'

'And why were you not at school?' demanded Mr Ramsbottom, turning his attention back to Elfie.

'I were in an orphanage,' she said, thinking she should probably have said 'was'. This was getting worse every minute! She was letting everybody down. They might fail! And then Pa wouldn't be allowed to teach them any more and they'd have to go to the normal school and they'd all hate her!

'Surely you were sent to school from the orphanage?'

'Well, I weren't there very long.' Elfie was feeling more and more uncomfortable. Staring down at the man's feet she saw that the spots on his spats were grease stains.

'And, pray, where were you then?'

'Might we have a word, Mr Ramsbottom?' said Pa, motioning him aside.

They withdrew to the corridor.

'Trust you to let us down,' whispered Ivy.

'She hasn't!' said Joe.

The two men returned and the interrogation

continued for another hour, after which Pa ushered Mr Ramsbottom out. The children collapsed with relief.

'What a 'orrible man!' declared Elfie.

'*Horrible*,' said Pa, returning just in time to catch her remark, but he smiled and everyone laughed.

'Will it be all right?' asked Elfie anxiously.

'We shan't know until Mr Ramsbottom writes his report.'

'If we don't pass it'll be 'er fault,' said Ivy, turning on Elfie.

'That is quite unfair, Ivy,' said Pa. 'We shall be judged as a whole. And Elfie did nothing wrong.'

'She recited that silly old poem.'

'It ain't silly!'

'*Isn't*,' said Pa. 'Let us think no more about it in the meantime. I feel confident that our standard is considerably higher than most schools in the borough.'

In spite of what he'd said, Elfie couldn't help feeling worried. The trouble was that she thought Ivy might be right.

After a morning like that, an afternoon doing deliveries, even in bucketing rain, seemed like a treat.

Elfie set off happily with the two boys. When Billy had been told she was going with him and Joe he'd said, 'She'll be a fat lot o' use. She's got arms like sticks.'

Elfie hadn't let that pass. 'What a cheek! You've not got much muscles yourself.'

Ma had stepped in. 'Skedaddle! Get on with your jobs and no squabbling! I don't know what's got into you kids these days.'

Their first job was delivering sacks of potatoes, carrots and parsnips, strings of onions, and cartons of cabbages and cauliflowers for a greengrocer. The man in the long brown apron sorting them out also remarked on Elfie's strength, or lack of it.

'She's a right skinny one,' he said, eyeing her dubiously. 'She'll never push a cart.'

'She's coming with me,' said Joe.

Elfie helped load up the carts. The stuff was heavy but she struggled on with it, staggering under the weight of the potato sacks and relieved when she managed to dump one into the cart. When it was piled high they set off, with Joe gripping the handles. At the corner they parted from Billy, who was going in a different direction.

After that, they had orders to deliver for an ironmonger and then a builder's yard.

Elfie felt dog-tired by the time they headed home but she wasn't going to admit to it to anyone.

Florrie signalled to her when they came in.

'My friend Pam knows where *Happy Land* is. She's never actually been there herself but she says it's at King's Cross, not too far from the station.'

'You're not really thinking of going, are you?' said Joe, looking at Elfie.

She shrugged.

Florrie gave Elfie the ticket back, then she said, 'I've been thinking about your roses and violets card and I can't help wondering if Alfred might have picked it because your mum's name was either Rose or Violet.'

After supper Elfie put the idea to Pa.

'We've had a number of Roses and Violets over the years, have we not, Ma?' he said. 'Let us go upstairs and take a look in our admissions register.'

Ma asked Mabel to keep an eye on the little ones and went with Pa and Elfie.

Pa took a book with stiff, marbled covers out of a cupboard and laid it on his desk. Inside, page after page was filled with his beautiful copperplate writing.

'We keep a full record of every orphan that comes to us, Elfie, with details of how they arrived, and with whom, if anyone. Also, the date when they leave, and where they go. Look, on this last page, is your record! You are the latest addition.' Pa read it to her: 'Elfrieda, usually known as Elfie, arrived 1st January 1900, accompanied by PC O'Dowd.'

Elfie felt funny hearing that read out.

'Turn back to the beginning, Pa,' said Ma.

The first orphan recorded was Mary Anne Magee, who'd been admitted to the *Pig and Whistle* on the tenth of April 1870, aged four years, of Irish parentage.

'That's how we come to start,' said Ma. 'She was the daughter of an ould friend of mine from Cork. And the very next day didn't Pa come across a poor wee lad crying his heart out in the street with nowhere to go so we took him in and all.'

'Mary Anne is a married woman in her thirties now,' said Pa.

'Indeed she is,' added Ma. 'With four darlin' babbies. She comes to see us every now and then.'

Pa was running his finger down the lists. He stopped. 'Now here is a Rose. Rose Watkins.'

'Can't be her,' said Ma. 'She's living up north. She sent us a card last Christmas.'

'I've found a Violet. No surname recorded. 1874, aged seven.'

Ma took a squint at the book.

'That's Vi with the flaming-red hair. She's got a good position as a housekeeper in a big house in York. We heard from her too at Christmas.'

Pa continued to scan the pages. 'What about Violet Drummond?'

Ma frowned. 'We haven't had any word from her in many a long year. Funny, I was just thinking of her the other day and wondering how she was doing.'

'I see that she came to us in 1880, aged ten, brought by her mother, who was ailing and couldn't look after her. The father had died in a mine accident up in Scotland.'

'Scotland,' repeated Ma. 'Didn't you have a thistle brooch in your bag, luv? When I saw it I thought it looked Scottish.'

Elfie found it.

'Well, Violet *could* be a possibility.' Pa sounded dubious. 'We have no real evidence to go on, however.'

'She was fond of us,' said Ma. 'She always used to come by and see how we were doing. It's not like her, not to have stayed in touch.'

'That's true,' said Pa slowly.

Elfie was holding her breath, afraid to speak, afraid almost to breathe. Her mum might have been called Violet! She'd hated having a mum without a name. It was if she had never existed.

'Elfie was born in 1888,' said Pa, 'so at that point Violet Drummond would have been eighteen.'

'The only thing,' said Ma, 'is that Elfie doesn't look a mortal bit like her.'

'What was she like?' asked Elfie.

'She was a real beauty, wasn't she, Pa, with peachy skin and blonde wavy hair? And she had a lovely nature to match. Never a harsh word for anyone. Never lost her rag. An angel, if ever there was one.'

Elfie folded her arms and scowled at the card. All right, so sometimes she might get a bit worked up. That's what Ma was hinting at, wasn't she? That she didn't have a sweet nature and she was no angel.

'But, of course, Elfie *could* take after her father,' said Pa. 'We must remember that. So we cannot rule Violet Drummond out.'

Screams erupted from down below, followed by shouts, and then more screams. Cuddles, who had a loud voice for his young age, could be heard above all the others. He was good at getting his own way.

'Lord save us!' cried Ma and she went hurrying off

down the stairs to see what was going on.

'Well, I think that is as far as we can get just now, Elfie,' said Pa. 'We have unearthed a few possibilities at least. This is akin to a jigsaw. We have to put together all the pieces we can find in the hope of building up a complete picture in the end.'

Elfie replaced the brooch in her bag, along with the card.

Tomorrow, after they'd done their rounds, she was going to ask Joe to help her find *Happy Land*. There might be somebody at the dance hall who'd remember Violet Drummond. It was worth a try. Anything was. She wasn't going to just sit here and do nothing while letters trailed to and fro across the Atlantic Ocean.

Chapter Eleven: Looking for Happy Land

'Why should you get to go out with the boys?' demanded Ivy. 'I 'ate sewing on buttons and I 'ate Miss Primpton.'

'But you're good at sewing,' said Elfie, trying to keep a straight face.

'It ain't fair. I'm going to ask Ma if we can swap today.'

'But I can't do buttons!' said Elfie, getting heated now. She'd *got* to go out with the boys. She needed Joe to help her find *Happy Land*. And she was blowed if she was going to go back to that mangy old shirt factory and that horror who rapped you on the shoulder with a thimble every time she went by.

'Time you learnt then, ain't it?' said Ivy and she marched off to the kitchen to look for Ma. Elfie followed in her wake, ready to fight her corner.

Ma stood firm. She was sorry, for she knew the shirt factory was not a particularly nice place, but Ivy would have to go with Mabel. They all had to earn something towards their keep.

'What's she doing?' Ivy whipped round to face Elfie.

'She's delivering. It's hard work humpin' stuff about.'

'I bet the boys do it for her.'

'No, they don't!' cried Elfie.

'Joe tells me she does her bit,' said Ma.

'Joe always takes her side.'

'I think we've had enough of this conversation, Ivy,' said Ma. 'I am trying to get you and Mabel a position in a smaller sewing workroom where Mrs Mullins, the woman in charge, is very pleasant. You would be sewing lace on pillow cases.'

Ivy looked slightly mollified though she was obviously still in a huff and gave Elfie a dirty look when she and Mabel set out for the shirt factory after lunch.

Elfie skipped along the street beside Joe and Billy. Their work was much the same as the day before. Elfie toiled on, determined that no one would be able to say she wasn't doing her share.

After the first delivery she and Joe rested for a few minutes in the shelter of a doorway. It was raining again.

Elfie had her chance now to speak to Joe on his own.

'Would you go with me to help find *Happy Land*?'

'It's a long way. Didn't Florrie say it was near King's Cross?'

'Billy might want to go and see the trains. He says it's easy to get a lift on a cart.'

'I don't know what good it'd do, Elfie.'

'I want to ask them if they'd ever knew Violet Drummond.'

'*Known*,' said Joe. 'The place might not be open in the afternoon.'

'I just want to see it,' she said stubbornly. Surely this must be the place where her parents had met! 'Just to see it,' she pleaded. '*Please*, Joe!'

'Well, I dunno. It'd take a while for us to go there and back.'

'We could hurry up with the deliveries. I'll work extra hard. *Please, please, please*. Else I'll go on my own.'

'You can't do that.'

'I will, if you don't come.'

'That's blackmail.' He sighed. 'We'll have to see how we get on.'

They had several more runs to do for a grocer and a short one for a chemist. Elfie kept her promise and worked hard, lugging the packages about, not complaining, and managed to drop only one, which left but a small dent on the package.

'That seems to be it,' said Joe finally.

'Can we go?'

'I suppose so. I don't want you going all that way on your own.'

Elfie had often been much further on her own but she didn't tell him that.

They'd arranged to meet up with Billy on a corner. He was already waiting for them, kicking an old tin can along the gutter.

He was not averse to the idea of going to King's Cross and he was pretty sure he could get them a lift on a cart along with himself. He knew one or two carters who went up and down that way regularly and were always willing to oblige.

They had to wait only a few minutes before a cart rumbled into sight. It was carrying firewood. Billy spoke to the driver.

'If you can find a space in the back jump in!' he said.

It was a jolting ride sitting perched on top of sticks of wood. They had to hang on to the sides of the cart. On one corner Elfie would have gone flying off if Joe hadn't grabbed her.

The carter dropped them off half a mile or so before the station. They thanked him and set off to cover the last part on foot. The rain by now had eased. Billy left them for he knew a short cut that would take him into the back of the station.

'Ta-ta then,' he said and went off whistling.

Elfie trotted alongside Joe, who walked with long strides. He was a tall boy, with strong limbs. Davy, one of the brewery drivers, had said Joe could be a boxer, he had the build for it, but Pa Bigsby said he didn't want any of his lads to go into the fighting game. He claimed it ruined their brains, getting their heads bashed about like that.

When they reached King's Cross they stopped. Now where? Roads ran off in all directions. They wandered about until they saw a policeman.

'*Happy Land Ballroom?*' said the constable. 'Won't be open at this time of day.'

'Don't matter,' said Elfie. 'We just want to see it.'

The policeman pointed along Euston Road and said it was in a side street. He couldn't remember which one exactly but it had a sign hanging out.

They hastened along the road, pausing at every corner to look along the side street, and when Elfie was beginning to think they'd never find the place they saw a sign swaying in the wind.

'What does it say?' she asked.

'*Happy Land Ballroom!*' said Joe.

Elfie cheered and broke into a run.

Up close they saw that the sign was decorated with fading pink and blue balloons. It was in need of a lick of paint, as was the door, which was closed and barred. Not a glimmer of light showed anywhere. The ballroom seemed dead.

'The copper was right,' said Joe. 'I expect people only go dancing at night.'

'Florrie says some places have tea dances in the afternoon.'

This was obviously not one of them. It looked as if nothing at all ever went on here now. Joe thought the dance hall might have gone out of business.

Elfie banged on the door but there was no response from inside. She marched up and down the pavement, frowning, not ready to give up yet, especially after coming all this way. She went round the alley at the back. Joe followed. The lane was empty except for three rusty old dustbins. One was overturned. A rat emerged and scuttled out of their way.

Elfie stopped in front of a door which was as scabby as the one at the front. She tried the handle. 'It's locked!' She beat a loud tattoo on it, using both fists.

'It's getting dark.' Joe glanced up at the sky. 'We should be getting home.'

The door opened suddenly and a big, burly man with a thick beard appeared on the step. His sleeves were rolled up to show heavily tattooed forearms and bulging muscles. His hands were huge and hairy.

'What the devil are you two up to? Thinkin' of breakin' and enterin', was you? Well, I wouldn't recommend it.' He showed them his fist.

'What are those tattoos?' asked Elfie, squinting to get a better look.

He was taken aback. He looked down at his arms. 'They're mermaids, if you're wantin' to know. What's it to you?'

'Just wonderin'. Have you ever seen a mermaid?'

'*Seen* a mermaid?'

Elfie nodded.

'You're a right funny one.'

'Have you?'

'Well . . .' He scratched his head and Elfie wondered if he had nits too, like Mr Ramsbottom. She was hoping the inspector's scrappy wee beard might be infested with them and that they'd drive him nuts so that he wouldn't be able to write his report. 'I ain't sure as to whether they're real or not.' The man sounded bewildered.

'They're real on your arms.'

'I suppose they are, in a manner of speaking. Hey, what *are* you two doin' hangin' about here?'

'Do you work here?' asked Elfie.

'I'm the caretaker. I see troublemakers off the premises. So I'd advise you to scarper, the pair of you, right now, afore I call the coppers!'

'I was just wantin' to ask you somethin'. Have you been here for a *very* long time?'

'Right nosy parker, ain't you? What are you wantin' to know fer?'

'It's important. Cross my heart and hope to die, it is. I ain't lying, am I, Joe?'

'For your information,' said the caretaker, 'I have bin here fifteen year. We run a good establishment. We don't allow no riff-raff in. I've only ever had to call the police out couple o' times.'

'I think me mum,' began Elfie, and paused to take a deep breath before continuing, 'me mum used to come here, a long time ago.'

'A lot of ladies have come 'ere over the years. Can't remember them all.'

'Her name was Violet Drummond and she had beautiful blonde hair.'

'Violet, eh?' He looked startled. 'I remember a Violet with blonde hair. Golden, it was. She worked here, must be twelve, thirteen years ago.'

Elfie was excited. 'That could be right.'

'Right pretty girl she was. Very popular, she had such a sweet nature.'

'What did she do? Did she dance?'

'She checked in hats and coats. Cloakroom attendant. That was when the ballroom were in its heyday.' He sounded wistful. 'Gone down a bit in recent times. Haven't seen Violet in many a year. How's she doin'?'

'She's dead.'

'Dead? I'm right sorry to 'ear that. I liked her.' He spoke fondly and Elfie suddenly wondered if he'd been in love with her mother.

'What's your name?' she asked.

'What's it to you?'

'It's not Alfred, is it?'

'No, it ain't.'

'Thank goodness,' thought Elfie.

'Can you tell us anything else about Violet?' put in Joe. 'Where she lived?'

The man shook his head.

'D'you know if she had a special friend?' asked Elfie. 'A man friend?'

'Not to my knowledge. Never knew of 'er havin' any men friends. She weren't like some of the girls, flirting all the time. She were more private. Kept herself to herself, though she were nice to everybody.'

'Why did she leave?' asked Joe.

'She weren't strong. She'd a weak chest, used to cough

a lot. I sometimes wondered if it were TB. That's all I can tell you.'

'Ta, anyway,' said Elfie.

'You don't look anythin' like 'er,' said *Happy Land*'s caretaker, before closing the door.

'Huh!' Elfie scowled. Why couldn't she have blonde hair and be beautiful?

'I'm wondering why she kept that special admission ticket,' said Joe. 'She wouldn't need one herself to get in.'

'It could've belonged to my dad?'

'It could. But it doesn't really help us find him.' Joe seized Elfie's hand. 'Come on, let's go! I might have enough money for us to go part of the way by bus.'

Daylight was ebbing fast; the lamps were flickering into life. This was Elfie's favourite time of day to be out, when the shadowy streets became mysterious, even magical. You never knew what might happen. Your pa might come strolling along the street swinging a silver-topped cane like Pa Bigsby's and he would come right up to you and say, 'You must be my girl Elfrieda. I'd have knowed you anywhere.'

They smelt hot chestnuts, and their mouths watered. There was a stand on the corner. The man was shouting, 'Hot chestnuts! Get your hot chestnuts here!'

Joe pulled a few small coins out of his pocket and studied them. 'I could buy us a poke. Would you like that?'

'Oh, I would!' cried Elfie.

The chestnuts *were* hot! They laughed at each other as they shuttled them about in their mouths, until they were cool enough to swallow. They were so immersed in the chestnuts that when they rounded the corner they were not looking ahead.

They ran slap into a band of kids bunched up on the pavement.

'Gi' us a chestnut then!' shouted one of the boys, and before Joe could stop him he had snatched the bag out of his hand and, throwing his head back, tossed a couple into his mouth.

'Thief!' screamed Elfie.

'My Gawd,' bellowed another boy, 'it's our Elf!'

Elf! The cry went up.

'Do you know them?' asked Joe.

Elfie nodded. ''Fraid so.'

They had no chance to escape. In a flash they were surrounded by a whirling, grinning, cackling band. Their faces looked wild in the lamplight.

'Who's that you got wi' you? Hey, darkie, is that black boot polish you got on yer mug?'

'You shut up, Froggy!' snapped Elfie. 'He's my friend and his name is Joe.'

'What colour blood you got, Joe? Black? Black as tar? Sticky too. Maybe we oughter find out?'

Chapter Twelve: The Fight

The gang moved in, closing the circle around them.

'I told you, Froggy,' screamed Elfie, 'shut up!'

'Always had a big gob on you, didn't you?' said Froggy. 'I'm thinkin' it could do wi' somethin' stuffed in it.'

'Get out our way!' Elfie tried to use her elbows but they were hemmed in too tightly.

'Listen to her! Our wee Elf telling us to git out 'er way! We thought you was our friend, Elf. Where you bin? You run out on us. What did you do that fer? And look at you now, all set up in new clothes. Where did you nick them from?'

'Gimme your coat.' A girl grabbed Elfie's sleeve and another one pushed in to give her a hand.

'Get off, Beryl!' screamed Elfie.

'I'm needin' a new coat. Hey, it's ever so nice. Got a hood too!'

Elfie delivered Beryl a kick on the shin and Beryl lashed out at Elfie in return but her feet were bare and did less damage than Elfie's boots. Elfie got in another kick but the girls wouldn't leave go of her coat and were tugging so hard that she feared they would yank her arm out of its socket. Beryl spat in her face.

'I'll kill you,' shrieked Elfie.

'You and who else?'

'Gi' us a bit of room, boys!' cried Froggy. 'I'm goin' to knock this darkie into Kingdom Come!'

The circle eased back to give him some space. Froggy was the gang leader and Elfie knew that whatever he said, went. He'd often bragged about 'knocking people into Kingdom Come'. Killing them. She'd always been terrified of him when she'd slept under the bridges. She was terrified now for Joe. Everyone had quietened and Beryl had a nasty grin on her face.

Froggy came dancing up towards Joe with his fists raised. Joe stood straight and still. Froggy lashed out, aiming for Joe's face, but his arms were scrawny and his aim wild. Joe easily ducked.

Snarling, Froggy came back, but Joe pushed him away with the flat of his hand and he went sprawling into the arms of his friends.

Elfie laughed.

'Git 'im!' roared Froggy. 'Kill 'im!'

They came howling like a pack of wolves at Joe, who brought his fists up and, in quick succession, laid out two flat on the ground. Elfie cheered. Some of the kids began to edge away, but one boy, taller than the rest, waved a knife above his head. Elfie screamed.

She saw the flash of the blade in the light as it descended. She watched, horrified, unable to move, as the sharp tip met Joe's cheek and drew a line across it, making his eyes dilate with pain. He put up his hand and liquid oozed between his fingers. He knew it was blood. So did Elfie.

'All right, break it up, you lot!'

The law had arrived in the shape of two constables, who moved in wielding their batons and straightaway the gang scattered, their rags fluttering in the wind, and within seconds they had disappeared like silent ghosts into dark alleyways. The street seemed suddenly intensely quiet.

The constables confronted the two left behind.

'So what's been going on?'

'They've cut Joe,' cried Elfie. Tears were streaming down her cheek. 'Can't you see? He's bleeding.'

One of the constables took a large white handkerchief out of his pocket and gave it to Joe.

'See if that'll help staunch the bleeding, lad. We'd better get you along to the police station.'

By the time they arrived the white handkerchief was stained a bright red. The sergeant on the desk said they should go to the hospital.

'They'll be worried about us at the *Pig*.' Elfie felt anxious about that, about everything. 'They won't know where we are.'

'The *Pig*?'

'The *Pig and Whistle*.'

'It's a pub up in Stoke Newington,' said one of the constables. 'Run by Ma Bigsby.'

'I know where you are,' said the sergeant.

'Perhaps you could get word to Constable O'Dowd,' suggested Joe, his voice weak.

'He's based in the station in Stoke, isn't he?' said the sergeant.

Joe nodded.

'He'd let them know,' said Elfie. 'He's our friend.'

'We'll see what we can do,' promised the sergeant. 'Depends where he is, of course. He might be out on the beat.'

One of the constables accompanied them to the hospital, which meant yet another long trudge through the streets. They were teeming now with people going home from work and vendors crying their wares. Elfie walked close to Joe. The sleeve was hanging off her coat but she didn't care about that. She was too worried about Joe. He kept telling her he was all right, but how could he be?

'It were all my fault,' she said miserably.

'No, it wasn't.'

The hospital was a big gloomy building that stank of disinfectant and people who hadn't washed for a long time. To Elfie, it smelt of death. Joe's name was taken and they were told to sit on a bench and wait their turn. The vast room was crowded with men, women and children sitting on benches. Most looked wretched and sat without saying a word, though several of the children cried from time to time and then their mothers did their best to quieten them. One woman was coughing so hard that Elfie thought she'd cough her guts up if she went on much longer, while a man beside Joe nursed a mangled hand. He was moaning. He said he'd got his hand caught in a machine.

The constable had to leave them to get back on the beat.

'I hope it'll be all right, lad.' He nodded at Joe's cheek. 'I expect it'll need a few stitches.'

They were sorry to see him go.

Elfie wondered how they were to get home. Walk, she supposed, but there seemed no point in worrying about that yet, for it looked as if they would be here for ages.

An hour dragged by on the big clock on the end wall, and then another. Elfie thought the hands must be working extra slowly. At times they seemed stuck. The patients shuffled up the benches each time a name was called out. The man with the mangled hand fainted, causing a stir, and was taken ahead of the queue, which resulted in some grumbling.

'I feel as I could faint dead away too, any minute now,' said an old woman wrapped up in a black shawl.

Elfie felt as if she could as well and there was nothing wrong with her.

At last, after three of the longest hours she could ever remember, it was Joe's turn. She wanted to go with him but they wouldn't let her.

She sat thinking about him and her blood boiled

when she thought of the gang attacking them, cutting Joe's face, calling him 'darkie'. A man, not a regular, had come into the *Pig and Whistle* one Saturday night and called Joe a whole lot of rude names and been shown the door by Pa.

'Any person who insults a child in my care is not permitted to drink on my premises,' Pa had told him icily.

The man, who was big and beefy, had gone meekly and never set foot in the *Pig and Whistle* again.

Elfie looked round and saw Pa Bigsby and Constable O'Dowd advancing up the room! She ran to them and flung herself at Pa who, in his lavender suit with his flowing white hair and silver-topped cane, was causing heads to turn. He was carrying his top-hat under his arm.

'There, there, now,' he said, patting Elfie on the shoulder. 'We're here to take you and Joe home.'

'He's in getting stitched. It were all my fault!' Elfie began to sob.

'I don't see how it can be,' said Pa, letting that slip of grammar pass. 'We will hear the full story later.'

When Joe appeared he was wearing a large dressing on his left cheek. He tried to smile when he saw Pa but it pained him too much. He'd had six stitches. Pa gave him a hug.

'Now let us go and find a horse-cab and get you home.'

In other circumstances Elfie would have been thrilled

by a ride in a horse-cab but all she could think of, as she was rocked to and fro through the dark streets of the city, was that Joe would be scarred for life and it would be her fault.

Ma Bigsby was serving beer with Florrie. They both dropped what they were doing and came rushing out from behind the counter to welcome them. The regulars joined in and from the passage, where they'd been lurking, waiting for news, came Billy, Ivy and the twins.

'We've been right worried about the two of you,' said Ma. She stopped when she saw Joe's cheek. 'Dear love you, child, what's happened to you?'

'He got his face cut and it were my fault,' cried Elfie. 'It were all because of me.'

'It was not,' said Joe again.

'They got caught up in a fight with a gang of street kids,' explained Constable O'Dowd. 'I know them. They're a bad lot.'

'But *I* knowed them,' cried Elfie. 'That were the trouble.'

Pa let those grammatical errors pass too. He said that the fact that Elfie had known those people once upon a time did not mean she was responsible for what they did.

'I'm goin' to go back and get them! I'll kill them! They've cut Joe and they've tore my good new coat and all.' She howled anew.

'That would not solve anything, Elfie,' said Pa. 'It

would make matters worse. They would come looking for vengeance in return.'

'What were you doing away down there anyway?' asked Ma. She and Pa gave the older children, Mabel, Billy and Joe a fair amount of freedom to roam about the town but trusted them not to go too far.

'We went to look for *Happy Land*,' said Elfie. 'I asked Joe to go with me, but he didn't want to. If he hadn't, he wouldn't have got cut.'

'You see, it is all 'er fault, ain't it?' said Ivy. 'We never had no fighting till she come here, did we?'

Chapter Thirteen:
Elfie Runs Away

Elfie sobbed in bed after everyone had gone to sleep. She cried because Joe's face had been slashed and his clothes bloodied. She cried because her new coat had a nasty tear in it. But she cried most of all because she brought bad luck with her wherever she went.

After Ivy had said that they'd never had any fighting before she came, Joe had said in his quiet way, 'That's not fair, Ivy.'

Pa Bigsby, too, had told Ivy off. 'You cannot lay the blame for what those boys did on Elfie.'

'But it wouldn't have 'appened if she 'adn't took Joe there, would it?'

'*Taken*,' had said Pa. 'Perhaps not. But he went of his own free will. In the end, it came down to misfortune.'

Elfie had seen that hadn't cut any ice with Ivy, nor Billy, either. He'd pushed past her in the kitchen later, giving her a filthy look. He and Joe were mates.

When she stopped crying she was surprised at herself. She'd wept buckets since she and Joe were attacked. It wasn't like her. The last time she remembered crying properly was at the orphanage when the matron had called her wicked because she'd stolen a piece of bread. She'd locked her in a dark cupboard for hours and hours. But those had been tears of rage. She'd kicked the door and screamed at the same time.

The tears she'd spilt tonight were different. They were sad tears. Sad because, deep down, she felt Ivy was right, for it was true that if she hadn't taken Joe to the dance hall they wouldn't have run across the gang. No one could deny that. And if Froggy and his mates hadn't known her they might have snatched the hot chestnuts and left them alone.

It was her fault that Joe had had his face cut and would be scarred for life.

She couldn't stay here and bring more bad luck to Ma and Pa Bigsby. She'd have to go.

She slid off her pallet and stepped round the sleeping bodies to the window. The street lamps shed some light into the room. Nancy was lying half on, half off her mattress. She was inclined to fling herself about at nights and sometimes she'd get up and walk in her sleep. Ma said it was due to bad dreams. Dora, next to her twin, was snoring, with her mouth wide open. Ma said that was tonsils. Ma had an answer for everything.

As for Ivy, she was sleeping on her front, which suited Elfie, for she didn't want to see her face.

She looked down on the street. There were blurred circles round the lamps like haloes. It was slightly foggy. Smokey, one of the *Pig and Whistle*'s kitchen cats, sneaked across the road, his long furry tail floating behind him. He'd be in pursuit of a rat, more than likely. Nothing else was moving. No carriages, no rattling carts, no dray at the kerb, no beer barrels rolling across the pavement. Nobody shouting or whistling. Eerie.

At least it wasn't raining.

Elfie gathered up her clothes, making as little noise as possible. They always had to lay them tidily over a rail at night, Ma was a stickler for that. She didn't want to think about Ma right now, it brought a lump into her throat. Or of Pa either. She lifted her boots and then she remembered her bag. She couldn't go without that, no matter what.

It was upstairs in Pa Bigsby's study.

Mabel stirred and half opened her eyes. 'That you, Elfie? Whatcha doin?'

'Goin' to the lavvy.'

Mabel closed her eyes again.

Elfie eased the door open, trying not to let it squeak. She listened. Nobody seemed to be moving. She tiptoed along the landing to Pa's study. The door was closed but it wouldn't be locked. He and Ma didn't believe in locked doors, not like in the orphanage. The matron used to carry a huge clutch of jingling keys at her waist. One good thing about that had been that you could hear her coming.

She turned the door handle and went into Pa's study. The bag was lying on his desk. She lifted it, took one last look round the room and quickly turned her back on it. She mustn't start crying again!

On her way down the stairs she was careful to avoid the steps that creaked. She paused on the next landing to listen before passing Ma and Pa's door. It sounded as if Cuddles, who slept beside them, was grumbling. He was cutting more teeth and was not his usual sunny self. That might mean Ma would be awake. He was beginning to cry. Under cover of the noise Elfie sped past the door and down the second flight of stairs into the kitchen.

Once her clothes were on she cut a slab of bread and a thick slice of cheese, wrapped them in paper and stowed them in her bag. The only money she had was the penny farthing she'd earned at the shirt factory, which Ma had let her keep. Something glinting on the shelf caught her eye. A shilling. Elfie slid her hand up and took the coin between her thumb and forefinger. She'd need money to get by. But, no, she couldn't do it, not steal from Ma and Pa Bigsby. She sighed and replaced the shilling.

Time to go! She couldn't stall any longer. She let herself out by the back door and dodged round the casks and barrels in the yard to emerge into the street. She could scarcely see across the road now; the fog had moved in since she'd looked out of the window. A church clock struck twice.

Elfie pulled up the hood of her thick serge coat and set off into the night. She wasn't afraid of the dark; she'd gone out in it ever since she was little. She didn't know where she was going, but certainly not down by the bridges, to join Froggy and his gang. They'd knife her too. She turned northwards, away from the town.

Seeing a nightwatchman swinging his lantern up ahead she slipped into a doorway. He had a dog with him. A nasty-looking cur. You could always tell with dogs. He was snuffling along the gutter. The watchman, if he were to see her, would ask her questions, think she was up to no good. That was what they all thought. If you were out after dark you must be bent on something bad, like a bit of thieving. Well, sometimes kids had to, hadn't they? She'd had to. What else were you supposed to do? Starve?

When the nightwatchman and his beast had moved round the corner she took off again. Once she got well away from the area she'd find somewhere to hole up for an hour or two and try to get some shut-eye. She could do with it. Her legs felt as if they were filled with sawdust but she pushed them on. There could be no going back. Elfie never went back.

The park was just visible ahead. She turned right, passed shops shuttered and dark, carts lying idle at the kerb, a stray dog out scavenging, houses with curtains tightly drawn. The odd sliver of light showed here and there. A baby might be awake. Or somebody couldn't sleep. Elfie thought of her warm bed back at the *Pig and Whistle* then pushed it out of her mind. She looked longingly at the chinks of light, wishing somebody would open their door and invite her in, for what was left of the night, and then she'd move on in the morning and not trouble them. But she didn't have much hope of that. And you always had to be careful. She was not so stupid that she didn't know that. Some men tried to tempt you to go with them; they offered you sweets, or the promise of a hot meal. She was wise to them. She could look after herself.

Her feet slowed, her knees buckled. She had to stop. Tiredness had come sweeping over her all of a sudden. She was beside a shop doorway. She moved in and settled herself down on the cold ground, resting her back against the wall, and within minutes was asleep.

She awoke with a jolt to find a stray dog sniffing at her ankles, trying to gnaw the laces of her boots. She shouted and kicked him off. He snarled but ran away.

She blinked. She had no idea how long she had slept but during that time the fog had thickened and was now covering the street like a thick fluffy blanket. She could see no more than an arm's length in front of her. It was as if she, and she alone, existed in this world. She shivered. She'd never minded the dark but she hated these thick, smelly fogs. Pa said they were caused by the smoke from the coal fires meeting the cold of the river. *Don't think of Pa*, she told herself. *Or Ma. Or Joe, either. Just don't!* She hadn't done any of them any favours, had she? And especially not Joe.

'Get up and move!' she said to herself firmly. If she didn't she'd freeze to death. That had happened to kids sleeping rough before. She struggled to her feet. Her arms and legs were as stiff and cold as boards and her neck felt as if it had been twisted. She lifted her bag and began to walk, keeping to the inside of the pavement, close to the wall

A little further on, the fog cleared a little and she was able to make out the shapes again. She had left the shops behind and was in a street of houses, each of a good size, not like the poor, narrow ones in the other end of the borough and over into Hackney, where up to a dozen people might be living huddled together.

A solitary light shone at an uncurtained upper window. A woman was standing there looking down into the street. Odd that she should be doing that in the middle of the night, but she mightn't have been able to sleep, or else wasn't feeling well. The woman waved. Elfie didn't wave back. She wasn't used to waving at strangers in strange houses. The woman disappeared.

A minute or two later, the front door opened and the woman appeared in the lit doorway. She was small and plump and looked as if she might be around the age of Ma Bigsby. She was wearing a mob cap and a wrap over a white nightdress. She signalled to Elfie to come across. After a moment's hesitation Elfie did so, hoping the woman might offer her some food, or money.

'What are you doing wandering about in the middle of such a night, child?' The woman had a kind voice. Elfie thought she probably would give her something. 'You shouldn't be out in this fog. It's bad for the lungs.'

'I couldn't sleep.'

'Neither could I! Would you like to come in and have some hot cocoa? I was just going to make some for myself. Cocoa with a nice slice of my special chocolate cake?'

The saliva ran in Elfie's mouth. It wouldn't do any harm, just to go inside for a half-hour and drink some hot cocoa and eat a slice of cake. She needed something to perk her up before she went back on the road. The woman had a round pink face and a dimpled smile and made her think of a rosy apple.

'All right,' agreed Elfie, 'but I can't stay long.'

'You may stay just as long as you like, dear. So do please come in!'

Elfie stepped over the threshold and the woman closed the door behind her. The house felt wonderfully warm and smelt of lavender furniture polish. A big clock in the hall was ticking gently. When the woman saw Elfie looking at it she told her it was called a grandfather clock. The large hands stood at five minutes to four.

'Do you have a grandfather, dear?'

Elfie shook her head.

The woman lowered her voice. 'Have you run away from home?'

Elfie shook her head again.

'My name is Mrs Duguid – we like to do good in this house!' She laughed. 'And what is your name, dear?'

'Elfie.'

'Short for?'

'Elfrieda.'

'I shall call you Elfie, if I may? Come along into the kitchen then, dear.'

Mrs Duguid paused at the foot of the stairs to call up, 'Ethelbert, do come down! We have a visitor. A young lady!'

So there was a Mr Duguid. Elfie felt a little uneasy about that but when she saw him come tripping down the stairs in his fawn slippers and dark-blue felt dressing gown she felt reassured. He was small and round, like his wife, and he too had a beaming smile.

'This is Elfie,' said Mrs Duguid.

'Delighted to meet you, Elfie,' said Mr Duguid, holding out his hand.

Elfie took it. The palm was soft and warm, and a little damp.

They went into the kitchen, prettily decorated with blue and white tiles, while blue and white patterned plates were arranged in neat rows on a dresser. Heat issued out from a black stove in the corner. It was a warm, cheerful room.

Mrs Duguid suggested Elfie might like to take off her coat. Elfie hesitated.

'You'll feel the benefit of it more when you go back out into the cold.'

Elfie allowed Mr Duguid to help ease it off her shoulders, leaving his wife to set milk on the stove to heat.

'Now then, Elfie,' said Mr Duguid, 'tell us about yourself.'

'Not much to tell.'

She didn't like questions. She didn't trust them not to go to the police and report that she'd run away from home or an orphanage. They would probably think they were doing her a good turn! There was something a little strange about them but she couldn't decide what. Odd, though, that they should both be up in the middle of the night. Of course neither of them might be much good when it came to sleeping. They seemed very wide awake. And sort of, yes, excited. They kept looking at each other and smiling.

She was beginning to feel uneasy again but she wasn't too worried. She reckoned she could deal with them if she had to. They looked soft in the body. A good kick in the shins should sort them out if they tried anything on. And then she'd be off.

'You must be able to tell us something,' insisted Mr Duguid. 'Will your parents not be worried about you wandering around in the middle of the night?'

Elfie shrugged.

Mr Duguid then asked gently, 'Are they dead?'

'My mum is but my dad's not.'

'Ah, so you do have a father. Where might he be found?'

'I don't know.'

'You don't know?'

'I ain't ever seen him.'

'You haven't?'

'But I know he's alive and I'm going to find him.'

'Do you know his name?'

'Alfred.'

'Alfred what?'

'Alfred T.'

'Alfred Tea? Like the beverage one drinks?'

'No, the letter,' muttered Elfie.

'So you do not know his surname?'

Elfie said nothing. She was glad to see a large cup of foaming milky cocoa coming her way. It was set down on the table in front of her along with a big slice of chocolate cake. She wouldn't be able to talk with her mouth full and as soon as she'd finished she'd be gone.

'Eat and drink your fill, dear,' urged Mrs Duguid, 'and you'll feel a lot better.'

Elfie lifted the cup and lowered her mouth to meet the foam. She'd never tasted anything like it.

'Good?' asked Mrs Duguid.

Elfie nodded.

Mrs Duguid smiled.

'Eat some cake too, dear. You need a little fattening up, I'm thinking. Look at those thin wrists of yours!'

Elfie looked at her wrists. She'd lay a bet that they were a good deal stronger than Mrs Do-Good's.

The cake was moist and rich. Elfie ate the whole slice and finished the cocoa down to the very last drop. Mr and Mrs Duguid beamed at her.

'It was a blessing that Mrs Duguid happened to look out of the window at that particular moment,' said Mr Duguid.

'It was the Lord who directed me,' said Mrs Duguid. Elfie stared at her. 'The Lord told you to?'

'Yes, dear, I talk to Him every hour of the day, and He said, "Look out and you will see a little girl standing across the street in need of your help." And so I did. And here you are!'

'Honest? You heard Him say that?'

'My wife would never tell a lie,' said Mr Duguid.

'What age are you, dear?' asked Mrs Duguid.

'Eleven.'

'I knew it!' Mrs Duguid clapped her hands together. 'This proves it, that it is the Lord's doing.'

Elfie stared at her.

'You see, we used to have a little girl, Elfie,' said Mr Duguid.

'Where is she? What 'appened to her?'

'She died.'

'She died?' echoed Elfie.

'Sadly, yes. She was never strong, not from the day she was born. We knew the Lord would let us keep her for only a short time. She came as a gift from Him. He who giveth also, at times, taketh away.'

Elfie was really beginning to get the creeps now. It might be a good idea to put her coat back on and get out of here as fast as possible but she felt too drowsy to make the effort.

'What age were she, when she died?'

'Eleven, just like you!'

'I ain't goin' to die.'

'You certainly are not. We shall see that you do not.'

Mr Duguid rose and took a small, silver-framed painting from the top of the mantelpiece and brought it over to show Elfie.

'This is our daughter, Arabella. Bella, for short. Bella means beautiful. She was very beautiful and now she is an angel in Heaven.'

Elfie gazed at a wishy-washy painting of a girl in a blue flouncy dress. Her dark hair was parted in the middle and done in tight sausage-like ringlets at the sides. Elfie didn't like the look of her. She thought her eyes looked mean but maybe it was mean of her to think that of a dead girl. Arabella reminded her a bit of Ivy.

'We have waited twenty long years,' said Mrs Duguid, 'but we always had faith that the Lord would send us a new daughter one day.'

Chapter Fourteen: The Duguids' New Daughter

Elfie awoke in darkness. For a moment she couldn't think where she was. She seemed to be floating in a wide, soft, warm bed, but she couldn't remember how she had got there. Then images began to flash through her head. A woman smiling, looking like a round rosy apple, waving. A man, round and rosy too, with a beaming face, wearing fawn slippers and a dressing gown. A large cup of foaming cocoa. A slice of chocolate cake. A girl in a picture, with ringlets at the side of her head. A dead girl. Arabella. Yes, that was what the man and woman had called her. Their name came to her too. Do-Good. Mrs Do-Good talked to the Lord and the Lord told her what to do. Everything was coming back to Elfie now.

She sat up and opened her mouth to scream, then closed it abruptly. Screaming might be the wrong thing to do. Better to keep quiet, not attract attention. She mustn't panic. She'd been caught up in dodgy goings-on before and knew that panicking didn't get you anywhere, except deeper into a hole. She could be crafty if she had to. Gradually, as her eyes were adjusted to the light, she realized that the room was not totally dark. A small blue night-light was flickering in a corner.

As she'd thought, she was lying in a big bed, with lace-edged sheets and pillow cases. A heavy smell of lavender hung over everything. Then she realized that she was wearing a white linen nightdress, also trimmed with lace. They must have taken off her clothes! She shuddered.

The light was too weak to make out any colours in the room but she began to distinguish shapes. A tall dresser. Pictures on the wall. Books on a shelf. A dress hanging on a hook. Dolls seated on the floor in a neat row. A dolls' house.

Elfie wondered if she might have gone through Alice's looking glass! Pa Rigsby had been reading to them from *Alice's Adventures in Wonderland*. At the thought of Pa, she started to sniffle, so she shoved him firmly to the back of her head. He wasn't here to help her. Nobody was.

She listened. The house was as still and quiet as the grave. Her skin crawled. She didn't want to think of graves or of the dead Arabella. She hoped Arabella's ghost wasn't lurking around.

She slipped out of the bed and padded slowly and softly about the room, touching first the dolls, feeling their cool porcelain faces, their blank eyes, their false hair; and then moving on to the dolls' house into which none of those dolls would fit. She took out each minute piece of furniture and held it up to the light. Little chairs. A table. A bed. A chest of drawers. She trailed her fingers over the dress that hung from a hook and discovered that it was made of taffeta and had frills around the hem, with small velvet bows up the front. It might have been a party dress of Arabella's. Elfie still felt as if she were in a dream, as if none of this was real.

She must get out of here! Fast!

The door. Where was the door? She fumbled her way around until she found it. But when she tried to turn the handle, it wouldn't budge. The door was firmly locked. She'd had a feeling it would be before she'd reached it. She was a prisoner in the house of Mr and Mrs Do-Good!

She'd heard of kids getting kidnapped before but not like this. She'd been taken by surprise. She'd never thought it could happen in a nice street of posh houses. Down by the river it was different. You knew you had to watch out for yourself there at night, even in the daytime. A blood-curdling story had been going round last summer about girls being taken away in a ship and sold for slaves. Once or twice a man had come up to her and asked her to come with him, promising to buy her new clothes and look after her. She'd not been such a fool as to be taken in by that. She'd run off each time, at the double.

Think! Elfie told herself, *think! And get a move on!*

The window! There must be one, surely there must. She groped back along the walls until her hands encountered the soft smoothness of heavy velvet curtains. She tugged them back and felt cool glass. Outside, a moon shone full and clear, all traces of the fog gone. Elfie looked down into a garden and made out the outlines of tall dark trees and fat shrubs.

She pushed the bottom half of the window up, just enough to be able to stick her head out and see that a drainpipe ran down the wall to the side of it. They were not very smart, the Do-Goods, leaving her in a room with an unlocked window. Of course they wouldn't be used to children climbing out of windows and shinning down drainpipes. Or would they? How could she know? She didn't know anything about them. But she did know that she had to get out of here as fast as she could. The window had no bars and was only one storey off the ground. A piece of cake. She remembered Mrs Do-Good's gooey chocolate cake and felt queasy.

Shinning down the drainpipe would be no problem for her. She'd done it often enough in the past. For a while she and Beryl and a couple of other kids had slept in a loft in an empty warehouse. They'd shared it with one or two rats but at least it wasn't as perishing cold as it was outside when frost lay thick on the ground. Then the police had come along and chucked them out.

First of all, she'd better get some clothes on. She couldn't go running round the streets in a nightdress like Wee Willie Winkie. After a few frantic minutes spent searching she realized that her clothes were not in the room. She'd have to dress up in the dead Arabella's clothes! She didn't fancy that much but she fancied even less going out in a nightdress. The drawers of the dresser were full of underclothes and stockings. And a pair of boots standing on a rack looked near enough her size.

Elfie was about to pull the nightdress over her head when a sudden thought hit her: in her trawl around the room she had not come across her bag! How could she have forgotten that? She couldn't leave without it. More feverishly now, she started to search the room again and in her haste kicked over a small box. She froze when it started to play a tune. *Twinkle, twinkle, little star, how I wonder what you are . . .*

She picked up the box and shook it hard but it went on playing its silly tune. On and on. *Twinkle, twinkle, little star, how I wonder what you are . . .* She'd always hated that song. They'd been taught to sing it in the orphanage, along with 'Wee Willie Winkie'.

Even with that noise going on and on, she heard the key turning in the lock. She froze. The door opened and in came Mr and Mrs Duguid, still in dressing gowns, still smiling.

'So you found the musical box,' said Mrs Duguid. 'Bella loved that box. She played it for hours, didn't she, Ethelbert?'

'She did indeed, dear. You seem to be a night owl, Elfie! Up with the dark, rather than the lark!'

'What time is it?'

'Midnight. Just a few minutes past.'

'Midnight?'

'Yes, you've slept for all of eighteen hours.'

'Eighteen hours.'

Elfie didn't know why she was keeping repeating what he was saying. It might be to give her time to sort out the muddle in her head.

'Did you have a lovely sleep then, dear?' asked Mrs Duguid.

'It were all right. But I want to go home now.'

'But you don't have a home to go to, do you, Elfie?' said Mr Duguid.

'Yes, I do. I live at the *Pig*.'

'The *Pig*?'

'The *Pig and Whistle*, at the foot of Green Lanes.'

'Is that not a public house?' said Mrs Duguid.

'What's wrong wi' that?'

'A place where men go to drink. A quite unsuitable environment for a young girl to grow up in.'

'Pa and Ma Bigsby are ever so good,' retorted Elfie. 'Pa teaches us all sorts of things. Poetry and Latin and Everyday Life in Ancient Rome.'

'Indeed?' said Mr Duguid. 'He must be an educated man. Strange, for a publican.'

'He knows everything there is to know in the world!'

'It's wrong to exaggerate, Elfie. It is akin to a lie. And that is a sin in the eyes of the Lord.'

'I ain't telling no lie. And I want to go home! Right

now!' Elfie raised her voice to a higher pitch. In a minute she might scream and when she started she could keep it up for a while. 'You can't keep me here!'

'Calm down, dear.' Mrs Duguid laid a hand on Elfie's arm. 'Let us find a shawl for you and go down to the kitchen where it's nice and warm.'

Elfie calmed down, for it occurred to her that she might have to bide her time, play them along, in order to give her the chance to think how to get out of here *with* her bag. For a start, she'd have to find out where they'd stashed it.

Mrs Duguid draped a soft woollen shawl around Elfie's shoulders and led her down the stairs. She went meekly and saw her two gaolers smile at each other. Thought they were smart, did they? Thought they'd cowed her? They'd soon learn.

They seated themselves at the kitchen table, with Elfie in the middle. Mr Duguid did the talking.

'We want you to know, Elfie, that we will not harm you in any way. Quite the contrary. I realize this may all seem a little strange to you but you have nothing to fear, believe me. We wish only to love and protect you and give you all the opportunities in life that our dear daughter was not able to enjoy.'

'Did you lock Arabella up too?'

'That was merely for your protection. We were worried that you might wake and go off into the night again. The night is dangerous.'

'So are some houses,' thought Elfie. At least streets

didn't have locked doors and you could run. Run for your life.

'Once we are satisfied that you have settled in,' went on Mr Duguid, 'we shall no longer lock your door.'

'That'll be never,' thought Elfie.

'So what do you say?'

'Dunno.'

'That's all right. We are aware that it will take time but we are patient people, Mrs Duguid and I.'

'And I ain't,' thought Elfie. She was going to get out of here before another day broke.

Mrs Duguid stood up. 'I think I shall make you a nice cup of hot cocoa to soothe your nerves, Elfie.'

Suddenly Elfie realized she was going to put something in it. A sleeping draught. She'd heard of thieves slipping them into their victims' drinks. She watched Mrs Duguid closely as she poured the milk into a copper saucepan and noticed that she had tipped in all the milk from the pitcher. Then Mrs Duguid turned her back and Elfie couldn't see what she did next but she could guess.

When the woman turned back again she was holding a large brimming cup of cocoa. Her smile was brimming over too.

'Here we are, Elfie.' She laid the cup on the table in front of Elfie.

Elfie stared into the swirling pale-brown froth.

'Drink up, dear,' said Mrs Duguid, hovering above her. 'You have had nothing to sustain you for more than eighteen hours. You must keep up your strength.'

Elfie lifted the cup and then, somehow or other, her wrist twisted and the cup flipped sideways and she was unable to right it and the liquid went flowing over the side to splash on to the floor.

'Oh dear!' cried Mrs Duguid, clapping her hands to the sides of her head. 'And I have no more milk left.'

'Couldn't 'elp it. It were hot and me hand slipped.'

Mr Duguid jumped up to move the chairs away from the brown puddle which had already begun to spread and Mrs Duguid went to fetch a cloth from the sink. Elfie took the opportunity to scan the room. And there, lying on a top shelf, was her bag!

She then examined the window. Luckily for her, the curtains were not drawn, so that she was able to see that it was a pull-down affair like that in the bedroom. And it was open a crack at the top, possibly to let out the fumes from the stove.

'Oh dear, oh dear,' Mrs Duguid carried on lamenting as she went down on her knees to clean the floor.

'It is all right, Elfie,' said Mr Duguid, sitting down close to her again. She could feel his breath on her neck. 'We would not think of chastising you for a small accident like that, especially on your first day with us. But you must try to take greater care in the future. We do not like to waste the Lord's provenance in this house.'

'It must be another sin,' thought Elfie. She had a feeling that the Do-Goods would have a big long list drawn up and she'd probably qualify for most of them.

'We follow what it tells us to do in the Good Book,'

said Mr Duguid. 'Spare the rod and spoil the child. We do not believe in spoiling a child placed in our protection by the good Lord.'

Elfie said nothing but she was thinking. Her head was working again at full tilt. If he imagined he was going to try to beat her he'd have a fight on his hands. She could fight dirty when she had to. She would kick him where it would most hurt.

'What are we going to give you to drink now, child?' asked Mrs Duguid, once she was back on her feet.

'Water'll do.'

'And what abut a nice piece of chocolate cake? You did enjoy it last night, didn't you?'

'I'd sooner have bread and butter or bread and dripping. My stomach doesn't do well with rich things. I throw up easy, like.'

She was given a glass of water and two slices of bread and butter and ate hungrily. She did need to keep up her strength. Once she'd eaten she yawned and said she was still as tired as a dog. They nodded understandingly.

'You've turned a big corner in your life, Elfie,' said Mr Duguid. 'You are bound to feel tired.'

Before they took her back to her room she visited the lavatory, which was on the ground floor at the end of a passage. She knew they'd be standing outside the door. This window, however, would be too small for her to get through. She might get stuck halfway if she tried. Besides, she still had to get hold of her bag. She sat on the water closet, her mind racing. On the way along from the kitchen she'd noticed a door at the end of the passage. It must be a door into the garden.

'Are you all right, Elfie?' Mrs Duguid called out from behind the door.

'Coming.'

'Wash your hands and face now when you finish. Cleanliness is next to godliness.'

They used to say that in the orphanage too. She'd often wondered if God could see if you'd washed your hands or not. You'd think He'd be too busy with other things. More important things. But she did as she was told. She wished them to think her obedient.

They escorted her into the bedroom, sticking like limpets to her the whole time, so that they were almost bumping elbows. She was about to jump into bed when Mrs Duguid laid a restraining hand on her arm.

'First we must kneel and talk to the Lord, child.'

They knelt down by the side of the bed, and she knelt too. They asked the Lord to protect her, to save her from sin and to make her a dutiful daughter.

'Amen,' they said in unison and then they rose, their knees appearing to give them trouble. They certainly wouldn't be able to run fast.

'So it's into bed with you!' Mrs Duguid pulled back the covers. 'We will waken you in time for breakfast in the morning. We won't let you sleep through another day.'

Mr Duguid lit the night-light.

'Our room is just next door,' said Mrs Duguid. 'If

you want us, tap on the wall. We are light sleepers, remember!'

'More's the pity,' thought Elfie.

'You don't have to lock me in this time,' she told them.

'Good night, child,' they chorused.

She was glad they didn't try to kiss her. She couldn't have stomached that. After they'd gone, she lay listening. She couldn't decide if they'd locked the door or not, her heart had been thumping too loudly. She waited until she heard them go into their room and their door close. Then she slid out of bed and went to find out it they had locked hers.

They had.

Chapter Fifteen:
On the Run Again

Elfie lay in Arabella's bed, flat on her back, keeping her eyes wide open, terrified that if she closed them she might drop off to sleep and miss her chance to escape. After what seemed like hours, but might have been only a matter of minutes, she heard snoring erupt on the other side of the wall. She had heard snoring before but this was deep and loud like the rumble of a train.

She eased herself out of the bed and yanked off the nightdress, letting it drop to the floor, and went to the dresser, where she took out a pair of drawers, a camisole top and a pair of thick woollen stockings. She must work quickly but quietly. She scrambled into the stockings, pausing every now and then to cock her head to listen. The snoring hadn't stopped. Now for the dress. She'd never worn anything like it in her life before. A party dress with frills and ribbons! The taffeta rustled as she pulled it over her head. It fitted. Her fingers struggled with the buttons at the back. She supposed Mrs Do-Good would have done it for Arabella. The boots fitted perfectly. Arabella must have been exactly the same size as her. Elfie shivered at the idea. Finally she wrapped the shawl round her shoulders and knotted it at the front so that it wouldn't slip off when she climbed down.

She was ready to go!

She pushed up the bottom half of the window but it wouldn't go the whole way. The gap was only enough for her to stick her head out. It would be a job trying to squeeze the rest of her through, especially when she'd have to find a foothold on the outside windowsill. And then she had to cope with the drop to the ground. She didn't want to break her neck, or her leg, either, come to that, for then she wouldn't be able to run. And she was going to have to run like blazes. She'd have to try the upper half of the window. It was open two or three centimetres at the top.

She dragged a chair across and climbed up, slipped her fingers into the open crack and pulled. Nothing happened. The frame must be stuck. It *couldn't* be stuck, she wouldn't allow it to be stuck. She wondered about kicking in the glass but that would make a racket. Besides, she might cut herself crawling through. She tried again, pulling so hard that her shoulders hurt, but the window moved just a little. She rested her arms, and tried again. Another small movement, and another, and then, all of a sudden, the top half of the window dropped right down, with a considerable thud. Elfie stayed still and listened. They were still snoring in the next room.

Quick as lightning, she threw her leg over the bottom half of the window. Her toe found the outside sill, slipped, and found it again. She clung on to the window frame while her foot searched around for the drainpipe. Something ripped, but she ignored it. She swung herself across and in a flash had her arms and legs wrapped firmly around the pipe. A short pause to get her breath back, and she was on her way down the pipe. She landed on the ground with a small bump. Now for the next window.

She ran round the back of the house, peering into windows until she found the kitchen. Again, the bottom part of the window wouldn't budge. She couldn't see anything to stand on so she had to scramble up on to the sill, using hands and knees. Standing on tiptoe she just managed to reach the top. This half of the window came down easily and quietly. Elfie vaulted over into the kitchen.

The moon was spilling enough light into the room for her to see that her bag was still on the shelf. She pushed a chair against the wall, clambered up and lifted it down. So far, so good.

She took a quick look inside the bag, checking that nothing was missing. Her father's letter from Canada, the signet ring, the locket, the painting of the *Pig and Whistle*, the newspaper cutting, the thistle brooch, the card that said *Roses are red, violets are blue*, the dance hall ticket, the brooch with the precious stones that spelt DEAREST. Nothing was missing. Not even the bread and cheese she'd packed in Ma's kitchen. The bread would be stale by now. She was going to dump it in the bin, then she thought she might be glad of it later.

Now she must scarper!

She scuttled out of the kitchen and down the passage to the back door, less careful about making a noise now that she was on the last lap on her way to freedom. The moonlight didn't reach here so she had to feel around in the dark hoping to find bolts. There didn't seem to be any. The door must be locked with a key. Her fingers located the lock but the key was missing. They must have taken it out! She wanted to howl with frustration.

The front door. She retraced her steps along the passage to the hall. Some light from the street lamps was filtering through a coloured glass panel, enough to let her see that the big wooden door was bolted top and bottom. She gave a sigh of relief and bent to undo the bottom bolt. It was stiff, but a good tug and it gave way. That left the top.

As she reached up she heard a noise upstairs. A door banged. A voice called. Another answered. Elfie dropped her bag and pulled frantically at the bolt, using both hands.

'Elfie, what are you doing?' cried Mr Duguid.

She glanced round to see him standing at the top of the stairs in nightcap and nightgown. She tugged again, using all her strength, and the bolt came back in a rush, snagging her finger and almost making her lose her balance.

'Don't go, Elfie!' Mr Duguid was coming running down the stairs as fast as he was able, his white nightgown flapping round his bare ankles. He was only three steps from the bottom step, now two.

'Don't go, Elfie!' cried Mrs Duguid, who was following behind her husband.

Elfie hauled open the heavy door. As she picked up her bag Mr Duguid came lunging towards her and caught hold of the back of her dress. She managed to wrench herself free, leaving him with a handful of taffeta.

And then she fled.

'Come back, Elfie,' he called. 'We only want to love you.' His voice followed her along the street. 'We only want to love you.'

She ran and ran and ran. She ran until she was out of puff and a sharp stitch in her side brought her to a halt. She leant against a railing, doubled over, gasping for breath. For a moment she'd been afraid her lungs were about to burst.

Once her breathing had quietened down and she could straighten up, she looked around. She was in a street that to her knowledge she had never seen before. She had no idea where she was or which direction to take. The moon had disappeared and it was starting to snow, small soft flakes that lay lightly on the ground. A mangy-looking dog came lurking around her legs. She gave him a swift kick with the toe of her boot and told him to clear off but he didn't, he came back growling. She tossed him a piece of her bread and cheese and while he was wolfing it down she escaped.

She must keep moving, she couldn't wait for morning light. The snow was thickening, the flakes blurring her eyelashes. She missed her warm serge coat. The shawl would soon be sodden and the taffeta dress was none too warm, as well as being ripped. She was glad, however, of the warm woollen stockings and the leather boots. As she walked she left footprints on the white pavement behind her. From time to time she glanced over her shoulder, in case Mr Do-Good might be following in her steps. But she could see no sign of him or of anyone else. The white, ghostly world around her was deadly silent. The street lamps gleamed faintly, giving her some comfort and stopping her from straying too wildly.

She wandered down one street, and then another, cuddling her bag close to her body, protecting it as best she could from the dampness. There seemed to be no houses on her right now, from what she could make out through the swirling, dancing snow. That, together with the darkness, was as bad as the fog. Could she have reached the park? She kept going. The snow slackened and suddenly she recognized a corner. She was at the top of Green Lanes!

Now she paused. She had been moving as if by clockwork, without thinking, but was she really going to go back to the *Pig and Whistle*? Would they want her? They had probably been glad to see the back of her. She'd let them down when the inspector came. She'd broken one of Ma's good plates. She'd been rotten at sewing on shirt buttons. She'd taken Joe into trouble and he'd got his face cut.

Then she thought of Florrie.

A few minutes' walk brought her to Florrie's lodgings. Florrie had shown them to her one day. Elfie stood in front of the house and gazed up at the dark windows. Not a peep of light was to be seen. Could she knock on the door and waken everyone up in the middle of the night? The landlady, Mrs Twitchett, might be angry and tell her to clear off. Florrie said she had a sharp tongue on her at times though her bark was worse than her bite. Elfie was getting wetter with every minute that passed and she was worried that her bag might get soaked too, along with her dad's letter, and the *Roses are Red* card, and the dance hall ticket, and the painting of the *Pig and Whistle*. Then the ink would run and the paint would run and they would all be ruined.

She looked round for a suitable stone, not too big a one, for she didn't want to break the window, only to waken Florrie. She rummaged about until she found one, then she stood back on the pavement underneath Florrie's first-floor window and took aim. The stone curved up and struck the glass and clattered back down to the ground. She waited. Nothing happened. Florrie had once said she slept like the dead, she was so tired after an evening on her feet behind the *Pig and Whistle's* bar. Elfie picked up the stone and had another try. On the fifth attempt she struck lucky.

The window went up and out popped Florrie's head, dressed in rag curlers.

'What's going on down there? Who is it?'

'It's me, Elfie.'

'Elfie! Good Lord! Wait a minute.'

Florrie's head vanished and the window came down. Elfie waited and after a moment or two the front door opened to reveal Florrie in her nightgown.

'Come on in,' she whispered, 'and don't make a sound or I'll have Mrs Twitchett after me.'

Elfie followed Florrie into the house and crept up the stairs behind her into her room.

Florrie closed the door and stood back to survey Elfie.

'Look at you! Dear love you! You're like a drowned rat. Where have you been all this time? Don't you know everyone's been half out their minds from worrying about you? And what on earth's that you've got on? You're soaked to the skin. Lord save us! Best get everything off and I'll find something for you to wear. Do you know what the hour is? Three o'clock of the morning.'

Florrie helped strip off Elfie's wet clothes and rubbed her down with a towel, then dressed her in a voluminous nightgown, and Elfie told her where she had been and what had happened.

'Oh my God,' said Florrie. 'Ma will go off her head when she hears all that! And Pa won't let them get away with it, you mark my words. Constable O'Dowd either.'

'Were they really worryin'?' asked Elfie. 'You're not lyin', are you?'

'I don't ever lie!' Florrie was indignant. 'Pa has been out with the boys and Constable O'Dowd from first light till dusk raking the streets for you. They even went down by the river to see if you'd gone back to any of your old haunts. Ma and I have been asking the customers to keep an eye open for you and to tell you to come back.'

'I dunno as I can go back, Florrie.'

'Why ever not?'

'I bring bad luck wi' me.'

'What a load of old rubbish!'

'Besides, Ivy hates me.'

'Ivy! She's only one person. Come on, get into bed, you're needing a good sleep from the looks of you. I'll take you along to the *Pig* later.'

Elfie, too exhausted to argue, climbed into bed beside Florrie and slept deeply and peacefully for the remainder of the night.

Chapter Sixteen: In Pursuit of the Do-Goods

In the morning Florrie told Elfie to stay where she was and keep warm in bed while she went down and had a word with Mrs Twitchett. There was frost on the window pane but Elfie was relieved to see no sign of a crack. That would have given Mrs Twitchett something to bark about!

'I hope she'll not be cross,' she said anxiously. She didn't want to get Florrie into trouble, along with everyone else.

'Don't worry. She's not a bad soul.'

Florrie came back with a tray on which sat a bowl of hot steaming porridge, a plate of bread and marmalade, and a mug of tea.

'She was as nice as pie when I told her your story. Thought it was shocking. She says Pa Bigsby will have to get the police on to it. People like that should be locked up.'

Elfie hadn't thought about the police but she supposed Mrs Twitchett might be right. She didn't want to think about the Do-Goods this morning.

'Sit up, then!' ordered Florrie, plumping up a pillow behind Elfie's head. 'You've not had breakfast in bed before, have you?'

Elfie settled back against the pillow. It was nice having Florrie fussing over her. She was starving too. Since running away from the *Pig and Whistle* she'd only had that slice of chocolate cake and the cup of cocoa. She ate and drank and Florrie watched approvingly.

'I'm going round to the *Pig* now to tell them you're here and fetch you some clothes. Mine would drown you. So don't move!'

'I won't run away,' promised Elfie.

'You'd better not!'

When Florrie returned she had Ma Bigsby with her. Ma wrapped her arms round Elfie and held her tightly against her warm, ample body, saying not a word. Elfie found she was sniffling again.

'I told you they'd want you back, didn't I?' said Florrie.

'We certainly do. What a horrible thing to have happen to you! You're a brave girl.'

'Trouble was they seemed nice to begin with,' said Elfie.

'And then you drop your guard?' Ma nodded. 'Let's get you dressed and take you home.' Florrie had brought clothes.

'I lost me good coat,' said Elfie miserably.

'Don't worry about that,' said Ma. 'Other things are more important. Joe's outside, by the by.'

'Joe?'

'He's been worrying about you. He thought you ran away on account of his getting his face cut.'

Elfie didn't say anything.

When she was dressed they went downstairs and sought out Florrie's landlady so that Elfie could thank her.

'Speak nicely now,' said Ma.

Elfie put on the nicest voice she could and said, 'Thank you very much. It were a lovely breakfast.'

In return, Mrs Twitchett said, 'Only too pleased to be of help, I'm sure, especially under the circumstances.'

Ma Bigsby also thanked her for her hospitality to Elfie and asked if Mrs Twitchett might be fond of the odd glass of stout.

'I'm partial to a drop, I won't deny it. I've been told It's good for the heart.'

'I can well believe it,' said Ma and promised to send a couple of bottles back with Florrie.

Joe was standing on the pavement, with his back to the house and his hands in his pockets. He turned when he heard the door opening. Elfie winced at the sight of the dressing on his face.

'Is it sore?' she asked.

'Not too much.'

Ma and Florrie walked on ahead, leaving them to follow.

'I didn't blame you, you know,' said Joe. 'I kept telling you but you wouldn't listen, would you?'

'But–' began Elfie.

'No buts. All right?'

'All right.'

She wanted to skip when she saw the cheerful old sign of the pig playing his whistle coming up ahead.

The whole household was waiting for them in the bar downstairs. They cheered as she came in and Cuddles laughed and clapped his chubby hands together.

Pa embraced Elfie and said, 'Welcome home, wanderer!'

She thought she might be about to cry again. This was terrible. She would soon be as bad as Cuddles!

'No need for any more tears,' said Pa. 'The main thing is that you are back safe and sound.'

They were being so nice to her! She almost wished they would be cross and scold her. The orphans had gathered in a ring around them. Even Cuddles seemed to sense it was a special moment; he was sucking his thumb and gazing up at Elfie. Joe smiled broadly, showing his dazzling white teeth. Mabel displayed the gap in her front ones. Everyone was smiling, except Ivy, but that didn't bother Elfie, for she knew Ivy had probably hoped that she wouldn't come back at all. She'd have felt the same about Ivy if she had run off.

'Let us go up to my study, Elfie,' said Pa. 'I would like you to tell me your story in your own words.'

She didn't want to have to go over the whole thing

again but Pa insisted. He said it was necessary so that he could decide what action to take.

Ma accompanied them and Elfie related everything that had happened to her from the moment she'd let herself out of the back door of the *Pig and Whistle* until she'd arrived at Florrie's lodgings.

'Dear love you,' said Ma, shaking her head. 'There are some right bad folk in this world and no mistake. It's a mercy you managed to escape, for we might never have found you.'

'They seemed to think they was doing good,' said Elfie. She was still puzzled by that. 'They said they only wanted to love me. But it gave me the creeps, just hearing them say that.'

'It's very sad,' said Pa, 'for they are probably not truly *evil*, though it is difficult to judge. I am inclined to think that they are deeply troubled people, and misguided. They wanted a daughter and thought they could give a homeless girl a good home. They may have seen nothing wrong with that.'

'But they kidnapped Elfie!' protested Ma. '*And* drugged her. *And* locked her up so that she couldn't escape.'

'All of which was very wrong of them,' agreed Pa.

'They're not the full shilling, if you ask me.' Ma tapped her forehead with her finger. 'They put Elfie through a dreadful ordeal, the poor lamb!' She leant over to give her another fierce hug, almost crushing Elfie's ribs.

'We shall have to report it to the police, of course,' said Pa.

'Do we have to?' wailed Elfie. 'I don't want to have to tell it all over again.'

In the afternoon Pa took her to the police station where they were fortunate to find Constable O'Dowd on duty. Pa had a few words with him on his own and then they went into a room with another policeman and seated themselves at a table.

'Take your time now, Elfie,' said Dowdy, 'and don't miss out any details, whether you think they're important or not.'

He listened in silence, pursing his lips, and at the end, asked, 'Would you able to find the house again?'

'I dunno. It were dark, you see, and snowing. And I don't want to go back there!'

'We'd be with you; you'd have nothing to fear.'

'That was what Mr Do-Good said.'

'You can trust me, Elfie, can't you?'

She nodded.

'We've got to track these people down. Like Pa Bigsby says, they could do it again to some other girl.'

Elfie didn't argue any more.

They set off, the three of them, with Elfie walking between Pa and Dowdy. The snow had not lain, except on the rooftops and in one or two narrow alleyways where the sun could not penetrate. It was a bright, frosty day.

Elfie was sure of the way only as far as the park.

'Can you remember which direction you came from when you got here?' asked Dowdy. 'Take time to think.'

She considered, then pointed. 'That one.'

'Let's try it then.'

While they were walking no one spoke so that Elfie could concentrate. She stopped after a few minutes.

'It might be one of the streets up that way.' She waved vaguely up ahead. 'But I ain't sure. It was foggy when I went and snowing when I came back.'

'Let's just stroll around and see if anything strikes you as being familiar.'

They walked up one street and down another.

'I'll never find it,' cried Elfie. 'This is 'opeless.'

'Did the house have a front garden? What was the front door like?'

'It was a big heavy wooden door.' But she could only remember what it had looked like on the inside. Once she'd got out she'd run like the clappers and never looked back.

They turned into another street.

'This could be it,' said Elfie doubtfully.

Then she glanced up and there, in the upper window of a house, was Mrs Do-Good looking down into the street, the way she had been doing the first time Elfie saw her.

'It's 'er,' she screamed. 'Up at the top!'

But by the time the two men looked, the woman had gone.

'It was her, I know it was her.' Elfie was shaking. Pa put his arm round her shoulders.

'Are you sure?' asked Dowdy.

'It were 'er! But I ain't goin' in, I ain't! You can't make me.'

'It's all right, Elfie, I'm not going to make you. You go on home with Pa and I'll go and interview the occupants of the house. I'll very likely ask them to accompany me to the station and then I'd need you to come and identify them.'

'I don't want to see them! I *don't*!'

'I'll be with you, Elfie,' said Pa. 'You'll be safe with me.'

On the way back they met Ma, who was out doing the weekend shopping. It was Saturday morning, Elfie realized. The days of the week had got lost for her. Ma had with her the old pram, whose wheel had been mended, and Ivy.

'Elfie identified the house,' said Pa.

'Good girl,' said Ma.

Ivy was looking the other way.

They parted and Elfie and Pa continued on to the *Pig and Whistle* and an hour later a summons came for them to report to the police station. The other constable brought it.

'They're denying everything,' he told them. 'Only to be expected. Doesn't mean anything.'

Pa had a thought. He said they must call at Mrs Twitchett's first. Florrie was at home; she'd been washing her satin blouses.

'That old torn dress Elfie was wearing?' she said. 'Why, I dumped it in the bin. I didn't think it was worth keeping.'

Pa asked Florrie if she could recover it. The taffeta dress with its velvet bows looked even more bedraggled now, having kept company with potato peelings and stained meat wrappings. Florrie, who had been holding it between two fingers, dropped it into a paper bag, and they went on their way to the police station.

'I'm a bag o' nerves,' confessed Elfie.

'You are going to be all right,' said Pa.

'Will they lock them up?'

'They would have to be tried in a court of law first and found guilty.'

When they arrived at the police station Elfie thought she was going to be sick. She also thought of turning and running but Pa kept a firm hold of her hand.

The constable went ahead and ushered them into a room, where sat Mr and Mrs Duguid at one side of a table, with Constable O'Dowd facing them.

Mr and Mrs Duguid did not even blink at the sight of Elfie; they stared impassively ahead. They looked like two china dolls, with their round faces and pink cheeks and ice-blue eyes, like the dolls in Arabella's bedroom. Elfie felt herself begin to tremble.

'Sit beside me, Elfie.' Dowdy indicated the chair next to him, while Pa Bigsby sat on her other side.

The other constable closed the door and stood with his back to it. There was to be no escape for anyone.

'Now then, Elfie,' began Dowdy, 'I want you to look at these two people and tell me if you have ever seen them before?'

'I 'ave!' she burst out. 'They took me into their house and put something in my cocoa that sent me to sleep and locked me in a room.'

'That is quite ridiculous,' said Mr Duguid in a soft, even voice. 'We have never seen this girl in our lives before, have we, Gertrude?'

'Never,' said Mrs Duguid. 'She is a total stranger.'

'I fear she is making up stories, Constable,' said Mr Duguid.

'Children sometimes do, I believe,' added Mrs Duguid.

'They said they wanted me to be their daughter. They said the Lord had sent me to make up for their daughter dying!'

'This is a preposterous allegation, Constable,' said Mr Duguid. 'You surely cannot believe that? I intend to make a complaint to your superior. For a start, we have never had a daughter.'

'Yes, you 'ave!' cried Elfie. 'She were called Arabella. I were in her bed. I seen her dolls and her music box. It played *Twinkle, twinkle*.'

'What a wicked girl you are to be saying such things!' Mrs Duguid threw up her hands as if in horror.

'It's you what's wicked!' shouted Elfie.

'Calm down a moment, Elfie,' requested Dowdy, 'till we see if we can sort this out.'

'There is nothing to be sorted out,' said Mr Duguid. 'We have been brought here on a fool's errand. But I fear it is you who has been made the fool of, Constable.'

'I may have something of interest to show you,' said Pa. He took the torn taffeta dress out of the bag. 'Have you ever seen this garment before?'

'It were Arabella's,' put in Elfie.

The Duguids did not blink an eyelid between them, not even then. They shook their heads, like clockwork dolls, from side to side.

'I think, Constable, that you have wasted sufficient of our time,' said Mr Duguid, rising and giving a hand to his wife to assist her. 'I suggest that in future you do not allow yourself to be so gullible and taken in by the lies of a wicked girl.'

Chapter Seventeen: Hunting Down Mr Primrose

For a moment after the Do-Goods had gone Elfie wondered if maybe what they had said was true. Maybe it hadn't happened. Maybe she'd been dreaming. But she knew she had not.

'It were them,' she cried. 'It's them that's lyin'. They did take me into their house and keep me locked up. They did, I tell you!'

'It's all right, Elfie,' said Pa quietly, touching her arm. 'I believe you.'

Elfie looked at Dowdy. Did he? He might think she was wicked and made up stories. Sometimes she had done in the past but not ones like this.

'I believe you too,' he said.

'But you've let them go!'

'I had no choice. It was your word against theirs. That's tricky. It wouldn't stand up in court. We have no evidence.'

'What about Arabella's dress?'

'They said they'd never seen it before. They said they'd never had a daughter.'

'And perhaps they didn't,' suggested Pa. 'That might have been a lie too.'

'But I was in her room,' said Elfie. 'Her music box played *Twinkle, twinkle.* They said Arabella had loved her music box.'

'It is possible that it was all fantasy on their part,' said Pa.

'You mean they might have made everything up?' Elfie felt more horrified by that idea than if they had really had a daughter called Arabella. 'But they'd have had to buy the dolls and the clothes and pretend . . .' Her voice trailed away. She couldn't imagine anyone doing all that.

'There's some odd people in this world and there's no denying it,' said Dowdy. 'I come across them in the line of duty.'

'Sick people,' sighed Pa. 'In a way one feels sorry for them.'

'*Sorry?*' Elfie could scarcely believe her ears. Was Pa saying he was sorry for the Do-Goods for kidnapping her?

'But it's all right, Elfie,' said Pa, patting her arm, 'I do feel sorry for you. Much sorrier.'

Elfie subsided.

'Trouble is,' said Dowdy, 'they might be sick but they can cause a heck of a lot of harm.'

'Indeed,' said Pa. 'They already have. I suppose you couldn't get a warrant to search their house?'

'Afraid not, with nothing to go on but Elfie's word.'

'My word's good!'

'I know that, dear. But I wouldn't be able to convince my governor.'

'But what if they take another girl?'

'Don't worry, we'll not let it drop. We'll keep them under surveillance. I'll make inquiries, ask the neighbours and the shopkeepers if they know anything about a dead daughter.'

'The death would have been recorded, presumably,' pointed out Pa.

'I'll check that too. I'll ask if anyone knows of any young girls being invited into their house. I've got to be careful. I can't accuse them of anything or I'll get myself into trouble. But if a girl goes missing their house will be my first port of call!'

Elfie had to be consoled a little by that although she was still worried. 'What if they come looking for me?'

'They won't. They'll only operate on their own territory. They're not like criminals who roam the streets looking for victims.'

Even so, thought Elfie, she wasn't going to stray far from the *Pig and Whistle* for a while, not on her own, anyway.

On the way home Pa said, 'You've got to try and put this out of your mind. It won't help to dwell on it and Constable O'Dowd will do everything he can.'

'I'll try.' Elfie did not sound too convincing.

'We still have research of our own to do, do we not, about your parents? While we wait for a reply from Penetanguishene.'

'If we get one.' Elfie wondered if Pa's letter had ever made it all that way across the ocean. The ship might have sunk.

'I've been thinking about the painting of the *Pig and Whistle*, and trying to track down the artist.'

'Would that help?'

'He might remember who bought it from him. Sometimes artists keep a record of their sales.'

They took out the painting when they got back. It was a little damp from its adventures in the snow, but, otherwise, not spoilt. Pa said he would leave it on his desk overnight to dry.

'Do you see a signature in the bottom right-hand corner?' He pointed it out. 'It says "Ralph Primrose". That is the name of the artist. And the date is 1886. I propose that we go on the hunt for Mr Primrose!'

They set off on Monday afternoon. Pa carried the painting in a thick brown envelope. 'To protect it from further exposure to the elements.'

Ma had excused Elfie from having to do any work. She'd said she'd been through enough of an ordeal and needed some time to recover. Besides, she and Pa were going out on an important mission.

When Ivy had opened her mouth to complain, Ma had given her a severe look and she'd closed it again. Ivy and Mabel were now being employed to sew lace on pillow cases for a Miss Swanston, who was much nicer than Miss Primpton. That wouldn't be difficult, to Elfie's mind. Ivy said Miss Swanston gave them Turkish delight every day when they finished. Elfie informed her that she didn't like Turkish delight; it was too sugary.

They'd had a recovery day on Sunday as well, for they were all at sixes and sevens, as Ma had put it, and the weather was nasty, so they had decided not to go out. Pa had told them the story of Joseph and his multicoloured coat and started to read *David Copperfield* by Mr Charles Dickens to them. After that Joe had taught Elfie to play draughts. He sometimes played chess with Pa. Pa said Joe was a natural player. Elfie considered Joe to be good at everything.

'Our first port of call,' said Pa to Elfie, 'is the studio of a Mr Fabian Summers. He is an old friend, and a painter. I am hoping he might be able to give us a lead.'

To reach Mr Summers's studio involved taking two horse-buses, since it was on the other side of the river. Elfie was delighted. Wait till she told Ivy! She didn't even mind that Pa wouldn't ride up on the top deck; he said it was too cold and windy and he didn't want to catch a chill. She didn't want him to catch one either. She enjoyed the rides and Pa let her sit at the window-side.

Once they'd dismounted, they had a little way to walk. Mr Summers's studio turned out to be a big shed in his garden. He opened the door to them wearing a smock that once had been white but was now multicoloured, like Joseph's coat. His hair stood on end, a bit the way Mad Meg's did at times, though he looked all there. He had a paintbrush in his hand. At first he seemed annoyed at being interrupted but when he saw Pa Bigsby standing in front of him in his lavender suit and grey top-hat his frown turned to a smile and he cried, 'Algernon, how good to see you, old friend! It has been a long time. Come in, come in!'

Pa introduced Elfie and while the two men talked, asking each other how they'd been, and how their wives had been, she looked around the room. It was a right tip. Dirty paint palettes lay about, and piles of paper, as well as canvases that were stacked higgledy-piggledy against the walls, while the floor looked as if it hadn't been swept for years. Ma would have a fit if she saw it. Elfie wondered what Mr Summers's wife thought of it, if she ever came here.

On an easel rested a large painting of half a woman with huge shoulders. He must have been in the middle of it when they arrived. Elfie didn't care for it much. She preferred her painting of the *Pig and Whistle*.

After some chat Pa got round to asking his friend if he was acquainted with a Mr Ralph Primrose.

'Not personally, no,' said Mr Summers, 'but I think I may know where he works. He shares a studio with the watercolourist Frank Flinders. Now let me see, I should have the address somewhere.'

He began to rummage about in the mess, pushing bits of paper aside and opening drawers. Elfie was beginning to think he would never find it when he suddenly cried out, 'Hallelujah!' and produced a piece of paper.

Pa copied down the address in his neat handwriting and picked up his top-hat.

'Thank you very much, Fabian. That is a great help. And it has been delightful to see you again.'

'And you too, Algernon. You must come again soon. Good day to you too, young lady,' said Mr Fabian Summers, giving Elfie a little bow.

'G'day,' she said and they took their leave.

'It is better to separate the words,' said Pa. '*Good day.*'

The other studio was by the river, not far away. Pa decided that they should walk; the exercise and fresh air would do them good. Elfie liked walking by the river for there was much to see, tugs chugging along, barges carrying coal, timber or bricks, some with washing flapping on deck, and now and then a bigger boat cruised past. When a barge passed loaded up with timber she thought of her dad but Pa said it was unlikely he would be working on a barge.

The only bad thing about the river was that Froggy's gang tended to gravitate to it, for they could always find things to nick. She didn't think Pa's silver-topped cane would be of much use if they met them. There was no sign, however, of Froggy or any of his mates. Being daytime, plenty of people were about: workmen, watermen, boatmen, strollers.

They found the address on the paper without any trouble and Pa tapped on the door with his walking stick. Nothing happened.

'He ain't in,' said Elfie.

'Patience. A painter cannot drop his work on the second.'

Pa tapped again quite gently, too gently for Elfie's liking, but after a moment the door opened and a man, smocked like Fabian Summers, though less messy, confronted them. His hair was neater too, Elfie observed.

'I am sorry to disturb you from your work,' said Pa, tipping his hat. 'But we are looking for a Mr Ralph Primrose.'

'That is I,' said the man.

Pa withdrew the painting of the *Pig and Whistle* from its envelope.

'That is my work.'

'I wonder if you would remember to whom you sold it.'

'Please do come in.'

This studio was tidier too, and the floor looked reasonably clean. A few weeks ago Elfie would not have noticed if a floor was clean or not. Living under Ma Bigsby's roof had changed all that.

Another man was working at an easel at the far end of the room. It must be Frank Flinders. He paid them no attention; he was too intent on what he was doing.

Pa introduced himself and Elfie and explained their business.

'Well, I think I can help you,' said Mr Primrose. 'I always keep a record of who buys which painting.'

He looked like the kind of man who would do that, unlike Pa's friend Fabian Summers.

Mr Primrose took a thick ledger from a drawer. 'I see that I did the painting in 1886 so I may have sold it that year, or the one after.' He ran his finger down a column and then stopped, saying, 'Here we are! "Watercolour of the *Pig and Whistle*, Green Lanes, Stoke Newington." I painted it because I liked the sign so much.'

'I like it too,' said Elfie. 'What does it say in your book?'

'That I sold it to Miss Violet Drummond on the sixth of August 1887.'

'It's my mum!' cried Elfie.

'Indeed? That is interesting. How does she do?'

'Passed away, sadly,' said Pa.

'I am exceedingly sorry to hear that. Wait a moment,' went on Mr Primrose, sounding mysterious. 'I have something to show you.'

He took a sheaf of papers from a drawer and began to leaf through them. He drew one out.

'She was such an attractive young lady that I could not resist asking her to sit for me. A young man accompanying her bought the actual painting, but this is the sketch of her that I did initially. He paid for the *Pig and Whistle* painting too. It was a present for her. I believe he may have been going away.'

'To Canada,' said Elfie.

'Indeed?' said Mr Primrose.

'This young man,' prompted Pa, 'would you recall how he looked?'

'As a matter of fact, I do.'

'That does not surprise me. An artist like yourself must have a good visual memory.'

Elfie was getting restless. 'What did he look like?' she asked.

'He was tall, with dark hair, and he carried himself well. He seemed very fond of the lady.'

'Was he called Alfred, d'you know?'

'I'm afraid I could not tell you that. But here is my drawing.'

Elfie and Pa bent to look.

'That *is* Violet Drummond, *our* Violet,' said Pa. 'We know it now without any doubt.'

Mr Primrose placed the drawing in Elfie's hand. She gazed at it and for a moment could not speak, she had such a big lump in her throat.

Then she said, 'She's beautiful, ain't she?'

'Very,' said the artist. 'You may keep it.'

'Do you mean it?' cried Elfie. 'For good?'

'Of course.'

'We shall pay you for it,' said Pa, putting his hand into his pocket.

'No, no.' Mr Primrose waved him away. 'I am more than happy to let the young lady have a portrait of her mother.'

Chapter Eighteen:
News From Abroad

'Now I've got a picture of both my ma and pa, like you,' said Elfie. She was showing Ralph Primrose's sketch to Joe.

Joe, like everyone else, thought Elfie's mother was a lovely lady.

'I don't look like her though, do I?' Elfie wished somebody would say she did, just a tiny little bit.

'Possibly not.' Joe was always honest.

She wrinkled her nose.

'You look like yourself, Elfie.'

'Florrie's goin' to put rags in my hair to give me ringlets.'

'I can't imagine you with ringlets,' said Joe, grinning and making Elfie pout even more, but it was difficult to stay annoyed with Joe for long. When he suggested a game of draughts she agreed.

'You've picked it up quickly,' he said. 'I'll have you playing chess soon.'

'You're just saying that.'

'Why are you so suspicious all the time? Come on, sit down, let's play!'

They had just laid out the pieces when they heard Dowdy's voice on the stairs. Elfie jumped to her feet, upsetting the board.

'He's might have got the Do-Goods locked up!'

Dowdy came into the parlour and joined them. He said straightaway that he was sorry, he had nothing new to report about the Duguids; they'd made no progress so far. They'd asked the neighbours, who said they kept themselves to themselves. The people on either side of them had been in their houses fewer than twenty years so they couldn't say whether there had ever been a daughter or not. The shopkeepers could not help either. Mrs Duguid did her shopping, paid it for it with cash, never asked for tick, and was pleasant and polite. A nice lady, they said. Mr Duguid was known at the dispensary and the ironmonger's. They thought him a real gent, with perfect manners.

'Huh!' growled Elfie.

'I know. We'll just have to be patient and bide our time. We're continuing to ask around.'

Elfie was sick of everybody telling her to be patient.

'I've got some other news,' added Dowdy. He looked at Joe. 'How's the face, lad?'

'All right.'

'He always says that,' said Elfie.

'You remember Froggy?'

'Wish I didn't,' said Elfie. 'I 'ate his guts.'

'We found him floating in the dock this morning.'

'*Dead?*'

'Oh, yes, dead all right,' said Dowdy. 'But he didn't die from drowning, he had a knife in his back.'

'I didn't do it!'

'Nobody's saying you did, Elfie. We know who did. It was another member of the gang known to them as Slinger.'

'He was the one that cut Joe.'

'I wondered if it might be. We've taken him in and charged him. The gang seems to have broken up, you'll be glad to know.'

After Dowdy had left Joe said, 'I'm glad he took you away from those people.'

'So am I.'

'It's awful, though, somebody dying like that.'

'But he were 'orrible, Froggy.'

'I know. But he didn't have much chance, did he?' Joe was wearing one of his thoughtful looks. 'I mean, nobody helped him.'

Elfie felt uncomfortable, for she couldn't help feeling pleased that Froggy was no longer alive and liable to jump out in front of her at any moment. Yet Joe might not like it if she said so, so she didn't.

'Poor folk don't get much help,' he went on. 'I've been talking to Pa about it and Pa says if I could become a lawyer I could do something to help them.'

'You're clever enough.'

'Problem is it takes money. And, well, Ma and Pa haven't got any to spare.' Joe's mood changed. 'Let's get on with our game!'

Elfie settled back into life at the *Pig and Whistle* again and after a few days her ordeal, as everybody referred to it, began to fade. It never went quite away and there were some nights when she'd wake in a panic thinking she was in the locked room with the dolls and the musical box. When Mabel sang *Twinkle, twinkle* to the little ones, Elfie had to clap her hands over her ears and beg her to stop. She never went further north than the park and even then only with Joe or some of the others. She worked hard at her lessons and Pa was pleased with her; he said her reading and writing were coming along extremely well.

The inspector's report came in. Pa's school had passed!

'Thank goodness for that,' said Elfie. If it hadn't she'd never have forgiven herself.

Whenever Dowdy came into the pub, which he frequently did, he'd shake his head, letting her know that they'd learnt nothing new. She was beginning to think they never would.

Dowdy and Florrie were walking out together every Sunday now. Elfie asked Florrie if she could be her bridesmaid when she got married and Florrie blushed.

'There's no question of that. He hasn't asked me, to begin with!'

Elfie made a note to tell him to ask Florrie whenever she got a moment with him alone. She thought he might be shy, not with criminals, but with girls.

Florrie tied Elfie's hair up in rag curlers a few nights in succession but Elfie's hair didn't seem to take to ringlets. It was too wild, said Florrie.

'Like its owner,' rejoined Ma.

'I've not been doing nothing,' protested Elfie. 'I've been good.'

At the end of the month they had a treat, a visit to Buckingham Palace to see the *Changing of the Guard*. They all went, Ma and Florrie included. They travelled by horse-bus. Elfie thought the guards looked wonderful in their red coats and big furry hats with the straps under their chins. She wished girls could get a chance to join. Billy said he fancied being a horse guard.

'No reason why not,' said Pa.

'I thought you was wanting to be a train driver,' said Elfie.

'*Were*,' said Pa. 'Billy doesn't have to make up his mind yet. His life is wide open. All your lives are, remember that!'

After the guards had trotted off on their fine horses, they stood at the gates and gazed through the bars at the palace, hoping they might get a sight of Queen Victoria. Pa said there wasn't much chance of that, she was seldom seen out now. The crowd grew excited when a carriage drew up and the gates were opened to admit it. They were just able to make out a man seated in the back and

Pa thought it might be the Prince of Wales.

'Our future king!'

On the way home, Ma bought them each a hot mutton pie, for it was a raw day and they'd got chilled standing around.

That Saturday night, Constable O'Dowd arrived at the *Pig and Whistle* as usual but, after a quick hello to Florrie, he went to speak to Pa. Elfie, watching from the hall doorway, wondered if he was asking if it would be all right for him to marry Florrie, but it seemed not, for after they'd had a word, Pa came over and asked her to go upstairs with them.

'I've not done nothing wrong, have I?'

'*Anything.* No, you haven't.'

They went into the empty parlour. The children were all downstairs waiting for the singing to begin in the bar.

'Our friend has some news about the Duguids,' said Pa.

'You've arrested them?' Elfie turned eagerly to Dowdy.

'No, not yet. But we've made a little progress. We've found a girl who told us that Mrs Duguid had come to the door one day when she was going by and invited her in. She offered her cocoa and chocolate cake.'

'The same as me!'

'Exactly!' Dowdy held up his index finger. 'But she didn't go in.'

'She weren't as stupid as me.'

'*Wasn't*,' said Pa and Elfie shook her head, annoyed with herself. She should have known that. She was doing her best to speak properly, like Joe and Florrie, but when she got excited she forgot.

'But you were out in the middle of the night,' Dowdy reminded her, 'and needed to find shelter. The other girl was walking past in the daytime.'

'They'll try again, the Duguids,' said Pa, 'from the sound of it.'

'I fear so. We can't do anything at present for they'd just deny it all over again.'

'They might never get caught,' moaned Elfie.

'Never say never!' said Pa.

'I knew you'd say that,' said Elfie, making him smile.

Florrie called over to Pa, 'This came in the post for you this afternoon.' She held up an envelope. 'I forgot all about it. I think it's a letter from abroad.'

Elfie stood stock-still. Could it be, could it be a letter from her *father*?

Pa took the envelope. 'It is indeed from abroad. That is a Canadian stamp.'

Elfie held her breath.

Pa turned the envelope over to read the sender's address on the back. 'And guess what, Elfie, it is from Mr Charles Devlin of the Georgian House Bay Hotel in Penetanguishene!'

Chapter Nineteen: The Letter

Elfie asked if Joe could come upstairs with them for the reading of the letter.

'Of course,' agreed Pa, 'if you would like him to.'

And so they assembled, Ma and Pa, Elfie and Joe. Pa sat behind the desk holding the sheet of white paper in front of him. Mr Devlin's handwriting was large and well formed so that Pa did not need his eyeglass.

This is what Mr Devlin had written:

> *Georgian House Bay Hotel*
> *Penetanguishene*
> *Ontario*
> *Canada*

> *31 January 1900*

Mr Algernon Bigsby
Pig and Whistle
Green Lanes

Stoke Newington
London
England

Dear Sir
  I thank you for your letter of 2nd January and take pleasure in replying.
  I am pleased to inform you that I may know the gentleman whom you are seeking.
  A young Englishman, Mr Alfred Trelawney, came to our establishment in May 1888.

'It's my dad,' cried Elfie, unable to keep quiet any longer. 'It must be!'
'It looks promising,' agreed Pa and went on reading.

  I see from my records that Mr Trelawney lodged with us for six months, after which he moved west. He had been sent abroad by his father to acquire experience in the lumber trade. I believe that his father was involved in the business himself.
  I am afraid I cannot give you any information as to his present whereabouts but I pray that I may have been of some use.
  Should you ever have occasion to travel to Canada we would be happy to receive you in our establishment and could assure you of excellent service and attention.
  I take the liberty to enclose a copy of our brochure.
  I am, Sir,

Yours most faithfully,
Charles Devlin, proprietor

The brochure was the leaflet that they already had.

'That's a nice letter,' said Elfie. 'And it was good of him to answer.'

'He's obviously a gent,' said Ma.

'The pieces are beginning to fall into place,' mused Pa. 'The only one missing – the biggest one – is Mr Alfred Trelawney himself.'

'I like that name. Trelawney.' Elfie tried it out in her head. 'Elfie Trelawney.'

'I suppose he could have stayed in Canada,' said Joe.

'Or returned to London,' rejoined Pa. 'We must act on that idea. Tomorrow I shall go to the library and look in the street directory and see if I can find a timber firm with the name of Trelawney.'

'I wish we could do it now,' said Elfie. It was always tomorrow. Why did it have to be? She hated all this waiting for time to pass. She'd like everything to happen NOW.

'It's too late today, I'm afraid.'

'Lord save us, if it's not suppertime!' said Ma, squinting at the watch pinned to her overall. She jumped up. 'Time we got the stove on. Come on, you can peel the potatoes, Elfie, and you can stoke up the fires round the house and bar, Joe.'

Complaining, Elfie nevertheless went, and as soon as she'd done the potatoes she ran down to the bar to tell Florrie her news.

She was so excited she could hardly sleep that night. When she left her bed in the small hours to go to the lavatory she disturbed Mabel, who sat up in alarm thinking she was going to run away again.

'Don't be daft!' said Elfie. 'I ain't runnin' nowhere.'

Pa visited the library the following day and consulted the street directory, but drew a blank. Elfie felt the dumps coming on.

'Never mind,' said Pa. 'All is not lost. A few firms have names like the East End Timber Company that don't tell you who the proprietors are. I propose to call on one or two and enquire if the name Trelawney means anything to them.'

'Can I go with you? *Please!*'

Pa looked at Ma.

'I expect she can be excused the delivery run. The boys can manage without her.'

'Very well,' said Pa. 'Tomorrow afternoon then.'

'Another tomorrer,' said Elfie, though she was slipping up less often now, for Joe always corrected her as well as Pa.

'*Tomorrow*,' said Pa and then he began to quote:
Tomorrow, and tomorrow, and tomorrow,
Creeps in this petty pace from day to day.

'But at least it does creep in,' said Pa. 'It comes, so remember that, Elfie! Do you know who wrote it, Joe?'

'Shakespeare?' Joe grinned.

'A good guess! It is from *Macbeth*. So, Elfie, tomorrow!'

And although it appeared to creep by, it did, as Pa had said, come, and Elfie set out with Pa to make enquiries at various timber companies, whose names Pa had noted down in the library.

'Don't know what you'd do without that library,' said Elfie.

'Neither do I!'

They travelled by horse-bus, and on foot. It was a fine day for walking. Spring, said Pa, was definitely in the air.

'It lightens one's step.'

The East End Timber Company yielded no information, and neither did the Riverside Lumber Company. The employees at both shrugged their shoulders and said they'd never heard of anybody of the name of Trelawney in the business. The proprietors had not been on the premises.

'Let us press on,' said Pa. '*Nil obstet.*'

By the time they had visited four establishments without success, some of which were at a fair distance from the other, even Pa's step was becoming a little less light. They took refreshment in a coffee house. After a moment's hesitation, Elfie ordered hot chocolate. Pa said she could not avoid it for the rest of her life. It would be giving the Duguids too much power over her.

'So drink it and forget them!'

After the first sip Elfie found that she had forgotten

them. Her head was too full of her father, Alfred Trelawney.

'I am beginning to wonder if the firm might be located somewhere other than London,' said Pa, 'which would be more difficult. We cannot comb the entire country.'

Elfie would be willing to, but not on foot. And carriages cost money. She sighed.

'We're not finished here yet,' said Pa. '*Nil desperandum.* Do not despair. We have two more addresses to seek out in the vicinity.'

Refreshed, they set forth again. The proprietor of the first company was in his office and invited them in.

'Now then, what can I do for you? Are you interested in purchasing some timber?' He looked dubiously at Pa's lavender suit as if he thought its wearer might not be the type of person interested in purchasing planks of wood.

(Pa Bigsby did have more than one suit. Elfie had found out that he had three identical suits, in fact, which allowed for one to be cleaned while he was wearing the others.)

'I regret not,' said Pa. 'We are seeking information about a Mr Alfred Trelawney, whom we have to reason to believe is involved in the timber trade.'

'I remember old Joseph Trelawney. A good sort. Dead now, sadly. It was an old established firm, Trelawney and Son. Joseph was the son, he inherited from his father. It was a good-going business in its time.'

'Was?' queried Pa.

'He sold up when he retired, seven or eight years back.

His son didn't want to carry it on. Disappointment for him, I think it was.'

'Children must be allowed to follow their own bent,' said Pa.

'You're right, sir.'

'Would you know if Joseph Trelawney's son was called Alfred, by any chance?'

'Couldn't really tell you. Might have been. I never knew the lad; he went to Canada for a bit.'

'That's him,' cried Elfie.

'And would you have any idea,' went on Pa, 'where he is or what he might doing now?'

'Why, I do believe he went into the law. Now I come to think of it, I'm sure that he did.'

'Do you have a street directory perchance? And if so, might I borrow it for a few minutes?'

'Certainly, sir. Only too happy to oblige.'

The man produced the directory and Pa began to turn the pages. Elfie clasped her hands together in her lap to keep them steady.

'Here we are,' said Pa slowly. 'Alfred Jonathan Trelawney, solicitor-at-law.'

'He's a lawyer,' breathed Elfie.

'His chambers are in Covent Garden.' Pa made a note at the bottom of his sheet of addresses. Then he looked up. 'I believe we may have found your father, Elfie.'

Chapter Twenty: Mr Alfred Trelawney

Pa said that he would write to Mr Alfred Trelawney and request an appointment.

'*Write?*' said Elfie. 'Can't we just go and see him?' If it were up to her, she would go right then. They'd wasted enough time.

'Absolutely not.' Pa Bigsby was adamant. 'This is a delicate matter and we have to tread carefully. Just think, if we were to go marching in and announce that we think you are his daughter! It would come as a great shock to him. No, I must see him first by myself and prepare the ground.'

Elfie had learnt that there was no point in trying to argue with Pa once he had taken a decision so she sighed and said no more, for the moment.

He wrote the letter as soon as they returned home.

Pig and Whistle
Green Lanes
Stoke Newington
London

Mr Alfred Trelawney
Covent Garden
London

Dear Sir,
I write to request an appointment at your earliest
convenience. I prefer, at this point, not to reveal the
reason for my visit, since the information which I wish
to impart to you is of a highly personal and extremely
delicate nature.

I am, Sir, yours, most faithfully,
Algernon Bertrand Bigsby
Proprietor

'If I mail it in the morning he will receive it by
teatime,' said Pa. 'We are fortunate indeed to have
such speedy postal delivery in the city. And then, if he
replies without delay, we should have his answer by the
following morning.'

A whole day to wait, and two nights! Elfie groaned.

'You'll have plenty to keep you busy,' said Ma. 'You
can go out with the boys tomorrow afternoon. They've
got extra runs to do.'

Not only did they have extra runs, but the loads, to Elfie, seemed extra heavy.

'My arms are killin' me,' she complained, when they stopped for a rest halfway through the afternoon.

'You could always sew lace on pillow cases,' returned Joe.

She leant over to punch him on the arm but he stepped sideways and she almost fell over. He kept a straight face. She made one at him and he laughed and his scar crinkled. For a long time the sight of it had upset her but Pa had said she must get over that, for Joe's sake. And she had.

'When I find my da I'll not have to put up with you any more!'

'Do you say?'

'I do. He's a lawyer.'

'What makes you think he'll want to see you!' Joe turned serious. 'You know, Elfie, you shouldn't count on it, for he might not.'

She looked glum now.

'But he might,' added Joe. 'Let's get on and finish the job. We've Mr Huckleberry to do next.'

Mr Huckleberry had an ironmonger's business in the High Street but today his wife was in the shop and looking fraught. A queue had formed at the counter and she couldn't find something a customer had ordered. She was talking non-stop.

'Mr Huckleberry is poorly. He's lyin' up there in his bed moanin' like a sick cat and my poor old mother's in her bed too. I was goin' to visit her this arternoon and take her some soup but I had to send my daughter instead and she's not come back and I'm near out my mind. She went close on three hour ago and I told her to come straight back and help me out here.'

Elfie perked up her ears.

The one woman in the queue tutted sympathetically and said, 'You know what young girls are like! They're easy distracted. My Maisie's just the same.'

The men were growing restless. One pushed forward and said he only wanted a can of turpentine. Joe found it for him.

'You're a great lad,' said Mrs Huckleberry. 'I could do wi' you givin' me a hand.'

'We've work to do, I'm afraid, Mrs Huckleberry.'

Two of the men left, saying they'd call back later; they didn't have all day to stand around.

Elfie moved in and parked her elbows on the counter. She lowered her voice. 'Your daughter – she's been gone three hours, you say, Mrs Huckleberry?'

'Now, Elfie,' said Joe, 'I know what you're thinking, but I'm sure there's nothing in it.'

Elfie ignored him. 'Where does her grandma live?'

'Her grandma?' said Mrs Huckleberry. 'Why, just on t'other side of the park. No great distance.' She mentioned an address that Elfie and Joe recognized.

'I expect she's met a friend,' said the woman customer, who had remained.

'I'd go after her if I didn't have to mind the shop.' Mrs

Huckleberry was eyeing Joe again.

'We're going that way,' said Elfie. 'We could call in for you, if you'd like, give her a message? Tell her you're needin' her.'

She was still ignoring Joe, who was looking at her with surprise, for they had no errands to do near the park.

'Would you, dear? That'd be a help.'

'What age is she?' asked Elfie as she turned to go.

'She'll be sixty-eight next birthday.'

'I was meanin' your daughter.'

'Marietta? She's ten, coming up for eleven.'

'Ten, coming up for eleven,' repeated Elfie, once she and Joe were out on the pavement.

'Doesn't mean the Duguids have kidnapped her!'

'It don't mean they haven't, either, do it?'

'*Doesn't.* I suppose not.'

'A walk round the park'd be nice.'

'Do you think so?' Joe glanced up at the sky, which was bulging with dark-grey clouds.

The rain started within minutes. It always seemed to be raining when they were out on their rounds.

'It ain't fair,' said Elfie.

'*Isn't,*' said Joe.

They found the house of Mrs Huckleberry's mother without any trouble, but they had to bang hard three times before she came to the door and then they had to shout before she understood.

'*Marietta?* Gone home.'

'When?' asked Elfie.

'When? Ages.'

Marietta's grandmother gave them a suspicious look and closed the door. They heard her putting on the snib.

'Now then?' demanded Elfie.

'All right,' said Joe, 'let's go back and see if she's home yet.'

They were both dripping wet by the time they arrived at the ironmonger's. Mrs Huckleberry was still behind the counter.

'She weren't there,' said Elfie.

'*Wasn't*,' murmured Joe quietly.

'But where's she gone?' demanded Marietta's mother. 'Wait till I get hold of her! I'll skin 'er alive!'

'I think you should go to the police,' said Elfie.

'The *police*? I don't know as that is necessary. I expect she's just been dilly-dallying.'

'Well, you see, I got kidnapped by these 'orrible people,' began Elfie, when Joe cut in.

'Maybe we should go and have word with Constable O'Dowd.'

Mrs Huckleberry was looking bewildered.

'Don't you be bothering your head,' Elfie told her. 'We'll take care of it.'

'I expect your daughter will be back before we are,' added Joe, which seemed to reassure Mrs Huckleberry more.

Dowdy, like Joe, was of the opinion that Elfie's

imagination was running away with her, since the girl had been gone only three hours.

'Must be four by now,' said Elfie.

'I'll come and have a word with Mrs Huckleberry.'

By now Marietta's mother was very worried. 'It's not like her, Constable, to stay away this long. She's a good girl.'

He said he'd call on the Duguids. 'But I'm going on me own,' he stressed, eyeing Elfie and Joe. 'You two wait where you are.'

He returned within the half-hour to report that Mr Duguid had answered the door and maintained that he had never met or seen a girl called Marietta Huckleberry.

'Course he'd say that!' scoffed Elfie.

'Nothing else I can do without a search warrant.'

'Can't you get one?'

'We'll give it another hour and see if she turns up.'

Joe went off to do a delivery while Elfie kept Mrs Huckleberry company. During that time she could not help but relate, or so she claimed, the whole story about her encounter with the Do-Goods, so that when Dowdy next came back he found Mrs Huckleberry quite demented with anxiety.

'You'll have to do somethin'!' she cried. 'They might be druggin' 'er wi' cocoa!'

'All right, all right!' He backed out of the door. 'I'll see if I can get a warrant.'

'It were the room to the right at the top of the stairs,'

Elfie yelled after him, before turning back to say, 'Don't worry, Mrs Huckleberry. He'll get them. He's a good copper.'

Outside the shop she bumped into Joe, who thought it was time they were getting home or else they'd have Ma out looking for them. They were in enough trouble as it was. They hadn't finished their deliveries and a couple of customers would be round at the *Pig and Whistle* complaining.

'We'll tell them it were a matter of life or death,' said Elfie. 'Anyway, I ain't goin' home till we see Marietta's all right.'

She headed off towards the park. Joe went after her. Ma had told him not to let Elfie out of his sight.

They waited at the edge of the park until Dowdy and his mate appeared and then they followed a few metres behind, stopping on the corner of the Duguids' street. Elfie would have carried on but Joe held her back.

'We don't want to mess it up for Dowdy.'

They watched as he went up to the Duguids' door and banged on it with the brass knocker. Nobody came. He knocked again. Still, nothing happened.

'They might have run off,' said Elfie.

Dowdy knocked for the third time and after that demanded in a ringing voice, 'Open up in the name of the law!'

That brought Mr Duguid to the door. He held on to the edge of it and peered out at the two constables. An argument then appeared to be taking place. Words were exchanged but Elfie couldn't make anything out.

'He's probably denying everything again,' said Joe.

Now Dowdy was waving a paper in the air. Mr Duguid tried to close the door but his toe met a constable's boot.

'That'll fix you!' said Elfie.

The policemen went inside the house and the door closed.

'I wish we could go too,' moaned Elfie.

They didn't have too long to wait before the Duguids' door opened again. Elfie and Joe moved up a little closer to get a better view.

Out came, first of all, the other constable, handcuffed to Mr Duguid, followed by Dowdy, handcuffed to Mrs Duguid. His other arm was round the shoulders of a girl!

'I told you, didn't I?' cried Elfie. 'I knowed it all along.'

'*Knew*,' said Joe.

Elfie and Joe were allowed to come into the bar that evening to tell their story. News had travelled and the *Pig and Whistle* was packed. The Duguids were in custody and had been charged.

Mr Huckleberry himself had risen from his sick bed to come and thank Elfie and Joe for helping to rescue his daughter.

'It's Elfie you should thank,' said Joe,

'Sometimes nosiness can be an advantage,' said Pa, smiling at her.

It had been such an exciting day that Elfie forgot, until the very last moment before falling asleep, about Pa Bigsby's letter to her father. As she drifted off she wondered if Alfred Trelawney would reply.

And if he did, what would he say?

Chapter Twenty-One:
Alfred Trelawney's Reply

Alfred Trelawney
Solicitor-at-law
Covent Garden
London

Mr Algernon Bigsby
Pig and Whistle
Stoke Newington
London

Dear Sir,

I thank you for your letter and would be pleased to see you tomorrow afternoon, Thursday, at 2 p.m., at my chambers. I pray that that may be convenient for you. If it is not, it would be possible to rearrange the appointment.

I am, Sir, yours most faithfully,
Alfred Jonathan Trelawney

'I shall go tomorrow,' declared Pa.

Elfie was so excited that for a moment she couldn't speak. When she recovered she put on her most pleading voice. 'Can I not go with you, Pa? *Please?*'

He shook his head. 'It would not be a good idea.'

'But what if he don't believe you?' Not that Elfie really thought anyone would disbelieve Pa.

'*Doesn't,*' said Pa. 'I shall take your bag, with your permission, Elfie, and show him the contents. I think they should provide sufficient proof in themselves.'

Ma excused Elfie from going out with the boys again on Thursday afternoon and gave her ironing to do in the kitchen instead, so that she would be at home when Pa returned.

'And I'm not wanting all me good pillow cases and sheets scorched! So just keep your mind on them, madam!'

It was a problem keeping your mind on stuff like sheets and pillow cases when it wanted to travel with Pa Bigsby to an office in Covent Garden. Elfie had been to the market at Covent Garden and done her share of thieving of turnips and the like. She didn't think Alfred Trelawney would be pleased if he were to know that, especially with him being a lawyer. But he needn't ever know it, need he? She'd rather he didn't know about her sleeping under the bridges, either, with Froggy and his gang.

Normally Elfie hated ironing but today she did not mind. She sprinkled the sheets with water and thumped the hot heavy iron over them, smoothing them out as best she could. When the steam settled she could see that the result was none too good. Not good enough for Ma's standards. She didn't know why they had to bother with all this when you could be doing other things. Like playing draughts or reading a book. She could read easy books by herself now. She wouldn't mind sleeping between crumpled sheets. But Ma would. And it was likely that Alfred Trelawney would. After all, he was a lawyer. Elfie imagined he would like everything to be nice and tidy. No wrinkles. No rumples.

She smelt scorching! When she lifted the iron she saw a large brown stain. Quickly she folded the sheet inward and hoped Ma wouldn't notice.

Pa arrived home as four o'clock was striking.

'Just in time for tea and crumpets,' said Ma, coming into the kitchen.

Pa took off his cloak and gloves.

Elfie dumped the iron down. 'Did you see him?'

'I did indeed.'

So Alfred Trelawney was real! They hadn't made him up.

'Me pillow case!' cried Ma, seizing the iron. 'Good Irish linen too! Ruined!' She shook her head but she said no more.

Pa seated himself at the table.

'Is he nice?' asked Elfie.

'He seems a very agreeable gentleman. He received me most courteously.'

'Did he believe you?'

'He did not attempt to dispute it. He acknowledges that the letter is in his handwriting, that the signet ring was his, and the picture in the locket was of him as a young man, and that he sent the *Roses are Red* card to your mother whom he met in the *Happy Land Ballroom*. He acknowledges that you may well be, indeed that you must be, his daughter.'

'Sit down, child,' said Ma, taking Elfie by the elbow and guiding her into a seat. 'You're shakin' like a leaf in the wind.' She set a cup of tea in front of her.

'Does he—' Elfie gulped. 'Is he wantin' to see me?'

'He has to think about it.'

'*Think* about it?' she cried. 'What is there to think?'

'You must understand, Elfie, that he has to accustom himself to the idea that he has a daughter whom he did not know existed before.'

'That'd be a shock for any man,' said Ma.

'He was very visibly moved,' said Pa.

'I'm glad to hear it.' Ma nodded her approval. 'I don't care for men who show no emotion.'

'There is a complication, however,' said Pa and he paused. 'He is married and has a daughter of six years.'

'He's already got a daughter?' said Elfie slowly. She'd never thought of that. Or that he'd have a wife, either. This changed everything, didn't it?

'Drink your tea, luv,' urged Ma. 'Nothing like a cup o' tea for steadyin' the nerves.'

'When he came back from Canada he went looking for your mother,' said Pa. 'That must be a comfort to you, Elfie. I believe he truly loved her. He told me that he searched high and low. He even came into the *Pig* one evening to see if she might be here, for he knew she'd been brought up with us.'

'Pity he hadn't spoke to us,' said Ma.

'We wouldn't have known where Violet was then either, would we?'

No, thought Elfie, for she was dead. Dead, dead, *dead*.

'He waited two years before he took a wife,' said Pa.

'A man of honour,' said Ma.

'But he won't want me, will he, not if he's got a girl of his own?' Elfie felt as if she'd been flattened by the iron. All the air seemed to have gone out of her.

'Let us wait and see,' cautioned Pa. 'He said he would be in touch. But he will have to speak to his wife first, of course.'

Chapter Twenty-Two:
Elfie Meets Her Father

Elfie's first meeting with her father took place in his chambers. Ma steam-ironed the red velvet dress so that it would not show the slightest wrinkle and Florrie put Elfie's hair in rags the night before, but by the time Elfie and Pa had reached Covent Garden her curls had bounced back into their old way. Not to worry about that, said Pa. He preferred her with curls rather than ringlets and he was sure Alfred Trelawney would as well. As a matter of fact, he said, her father also had black curly hair. That cheered Elfie a little.

'I'm a bag of nerves,' she confided.

'I expect Mr Trelawney is too,' said Pa, who kept hold of her hand all the way. They had decided to ride inside on the bus so as not to arrive dishevelled at the lawyer's chambers. Coming home, they might throw caution to the four winds.

'Honest? Do you think he'd feel the same?' Elfie found it difficult to believe.

'I am certain,' declared Pa.

When they arrived at the chambers they were admitted by a man in a black suit and starched white shirt with a stand-up collar. He had a starchy manner to match and little hair, but long ginger sideburns. Elfie thought for a moment that he was Alfred Trelawney. Her father! She was relieved when Pa said they had an appointment and presented his card.

'Mr Trelawney is expecting you,' said the clerk in a lugubrious voice after he had scrutinized it.

He opened a door off the hall and announced, 'Mr Algernon Bigsby to see you, Mr Trelawney.'

Alfred Trelawney had been standing in front of the window gazing down into the street. He whipped round to face them.

'Ah, Mr Bigsby!' He came forward to shake hands. 'How nice to see you again.'

He then let his eyes drop down to Elfie's height. He was, indeed, a tall man and he dwarfed both her and Pa.

'And this is young Elfie,' said Pa.

'Hello, Elfie,' said Alfred Trelawney gravely and extended his hand.

She took it in hers and said nothing. His hand was warm, hers was cold as ice. He looked directly into her eyes and she saw that his were dark brown, like her own. His hair lay low on the nape of his neck and, it was true, it was dark and curly.

'I am very pleased to meet you, Elfie,' he said.

She was unable to utter a sound.

He dropped her hand and invited them to come and sit by the fire. He remarked that although it was March the air was still chilly. Would they like to remove their coats?

He helped Elfie to take hers off and Pa his cloak and hung both on a stand by the door. Elfie smoothed down her red velvet skirt. They then seated themselves on deep red leather armchairs. Elfie sank into hers, finding her feet barely touched the floor. The fire roared and crackled in the grate. The brass coal scuttle, fender and fire tongs gleamed in its light. It seemed to Elfie that everything in the room shone, including the red chairs, the wooden desk and bookcase, both of which she knew to be made of mahogany because they were similar to the ones in Pa Bigsby's study. The carpet under their feet was a rich red. And she was wearing a red velvet dress.

On the walls hung paintings of tall dark-green trees and high, snow-capped mountains.

'Those are the Canadian Rocky Mountains,' said Alfred Trelawney. 'I think you know I spent some time in Canada?'

Elfie nodded. If she were to come to speak, which at the moment she could not imagine, she was going to have to be careful how she pronounced her words. There was to be no dropping of aitches or g's or saying of 'ain't'. She would not want her father to think she could not speak properly. On the bus Pa had told her not to worry about it but she was worrying.

A knock on the door, and the starchy man reappeared carrying a silver tray aloft. Elfie was amazed that he could balance so much on one hand without dropping it. Taking his time he set the tray down on a small round table in front of them. On it sat a silver teapot, with milk jug and sugar bowl to match, as well as fine china cups, saucers and side plates, and also a larger plate of cream cakes. The silver gleamed too now in the firelight.

'Will that be all, sir?' The man was standing to attention, like a soldier.

'Yes, thank you, Jenkins.'

Jenkins withdrew.

'Would you like a cup of tea, Elfie?' asked Alfred Trelawney. 'Sugar and cream?'

The sugar came in the form of lumps and Elfie wondered if she could sneak a couple into her pocket for Joe, who had a sweet tooth. She hesitated. Then, maybe not, she decided.

Her hands shook as she took the fine china cup and saucer from Mr Trelawney.

'A cream puff?'

Her mouth watered but she shook her head. She was worried she might get cream on her chin or drop a blob on her good dress. Ma was always getting on at her for spilling things.

He looked disappointed. 'Oh, come on, do have a cake! They were bought especially for you.'

She gave in. Pa suggested she rest the cup and saucer on the table while she ate the cake.

The two men passed a few remarks between them, something to do with the government, which gave Elfie a chance to take a wider look around the room. The first things she noticed were two silver frames standing on the mahogany desk, with their backs to her. When Alfred Trelawney saw her eyeing them he rose and brought them to her.

'This is my wife, Clarissa,' he said. 'And this is my daughter, Rosalind.'

The wife had golden ringlets clipped to the side of her head and she was smiling, resting her chin on one hand. The daughter also had golden ringlets and she too was smiling, showing dimples in her chin.

'I ain't goin' to like them,' thought Elfie. 'I just know I ain't.'

'Your daughter obviously takes after her mother,' remarked Pa Bigsby.

'Very much so. In temperament too.' Alfred Trelawney cleared his throat, then said in a husky voice, 'I rather think, Elfie, that you might take after me.'

She looked up into his face.

'We have the same hair. Difficult to tame, isn't it?'

She nodded.

'Shall I tell you where we get it from?' He sat down again. 'My grandmother, on my mother's side, came from Bermuda in the West Indies.'

'That's in the Caribbean, Elfie,' said Pa. 'Where Joe comes from.'

'He come from Trinidad.' *Darn!* Elfie scolded herself,

inside her head. She should have said 'came'. Now her father would think she was pig-ignorant.

'That's interesting.'

'He lives in the *Pig*.' Elfie's tongue suddenly became loose. 'He's my best friend. He sees me right. And he's ever so clever.'

'He is quite a remarkable young man,' put in Pa Bigsby. 'Intelligent and sensitive. I have high hopes for him.'

'He wants to be a lawyer, like you.' Elfie looked at her father. 'But he ain't got—' She felt her face flush. 'But he hasn't got any money,' she went on. 'He's got black hair too but his is crinkly and ours is curly.'

Ours! She would be able to say, 'My father and I both have black curly hair.' That would be one in the eye for Ivy. She would have masses to tell when she got back. They would all be waiting to hear. Florrie had teased her when she was trying to fix her ringlets into place, saying, 'Don't you be getting any uppity ideas now, just because your pa's a lawyer!'

'I'll look forward to meeting your friend Joe,' said Alfred Trelawney. 'And I would like you to meet my wife and daughter. Perhaps we can arrange a visit? For you to come to tea? Would Sunday afternoon suit?'

'Can Pa come too? Pa Bigsby,' Elfie added, for her *real* pa was Alfred Trelawney. She couldn't imagine actually calling him that, not out loud anyway. She might try it in her head.

'Of course! We would be delighted to receive you, Mr

Bigsby. Would Mrs Bigsby care to join us also?'

'It is too difficult for her to leave the house for any length of time, with so many children to attend to.'

'I'm not surprised. I don't know how you do it! Ten children, did you say?'

'Normally we have ten. But Elfie makes eleven.'

'I am full of admiration for you.'

Pa tipped his head, acknowledging the compliment. 'We enjoy them all.'

'Wonderful! I shall write out our address for you. We live in Hampstead, overlooking the heath.'

'A very pleasant place to live,' said Pa.

'We are fond of it. The air is good for children.'

When they had drunk their tea and eaten their cakes, Pa said they would take their leave now, for Mr Trelawney must be a busy man. Their host fetched Pa's cloak and Elfie's coat.

After he had helped Elfie on with her coat he stood back for a moment and looked at her.

Then suddenly he said, 'I must give my new daughter a hug!' and came forward to enfold her in his arms. He hugged her tight.

Elfie kept back her tears until they were outside the door.

Chapter Twenty-Three:
The Wife and Daughter

Sunday was a bright sunny day. White puffy clouds scudded across the blue sky above Hampstead Heath. Children flew kites, holding tightly on to the strings so that they would not be whipped out of their hands by the light breeze.

The Trelawney house was large and detached, and surrounded by a walled garden.

'Cor,' breathed Elfie, 'it ain't half big.'

'*Isn't*,' said Pa.

'I didn't mean to say that!' Elfie could have kicked herself.

'Habits take a while to change.' Pa smiled. 'I used to live in a house rather like this, when I was a boy, and before my father lost his money.'

The door was opened to them by a maid in a black dress and white frilly apron. She wore a black and white hat too, perched on top of her head.

'You're expected, sir,' she said, taking Pa's hat and stick. 'It's Mr Bigsby, isn't it?' She looked at Elfie. 'And Miss Bigsby?'

'Elfie is sufficient,' responded Pa.

Elfie handed over her coat, and Pa his cloak.

'Mr and Mrs Trelawney are in the drawing room,' announced the maid.

They followed her along the hall and up a wide staircase. Large, gold-framed paintings of people in olden dress lined the walls on either side. They were Mrs Trelawney's ancestors, they were later told. She had come from an old established family. Landed gentry. Pa explained that that meant they had a big house, with inherited land. Her parents had not been keen on her marrying into 'trade', which was how they had labelled Alfred Trelawney's family since they were in the timber business. She had gone against her parents' wishes and married Alfred. For love.

Elfie felt her knees quake as they neared the top of the stairs. Pa had said she should feel more confident this time, since she knew that her father liked her. That was all very well, but there was the wife and daughter.

The maid opened a door and ushered them into a high, light room. A glass chandelier hung from the centre of the ceiling.

'Mr Bigsby and Elfie,' announced the maid.

Alfred Trelawney sprang up from his chair and came to greet them. He gave Elfie another hug and then, keeping his arm round her shoulders, led her over to the sofa, where sat his wife and daughter.

Mrs Trelawney stood up to shake Elfie's hand. She smiled and said, 'Welcome to our home, Elfie.'

'And this is Rosalind!' Alfred Trelawney seized his daughter's hand and jumped her up on to her feet, making her laugh and her dimples deepen.

'Papa says you're my sister,' said Rosalind. 'But you don't belong to Mama, do you?'

Her mother looked flustered. 'We did explain it to you, Rosalind.' A blush had spread across her cheeks.

Pa had warned Elfie that it would have been difficult for Mrs Trelawney when her husband had come home to announce he had another daughter. Elfie must make allowances for that.

Pa Bigsby admired the room and the view from the window, drawing attention away from Elfie.

Mrs Trelawney pulled a bell on the wall. 'I think we shall have Ethel bring the tea. Do sit down, dear,' she said to Elfie.

Rosalind sat opposite Elfie, staring at her. Her golden ringlets were in perfect shape and looked as if they would never unravel even out in a high wind. She wore a pale-pink taffeta dress with spotless white stockings and black patent shoes.

Mrs Trelawney made a funny sound in her throat before asking, 'What school do you go to, Elfie?'

'Pa Bigsby's.'

'I didn't know he ran a school. Alfred didn't tell me.'

'It's only for us children in the *Pig*.'

'The *Pig*?'

Rosalind giggled.

'The *Pig and Whistle*,' said Elfie. 'It's a pub in Stoke Newington.'

'Oh, yes, of course. Alfred did tell me that.' Mrs Trelawney forced a smile. Elfie could see it was forced.

'I'm going to school soon,' said Rosalind. 'But not to your school.'

'We wouldn't have you,' said Elfie to herself.

Mrs Trelawney did another bit of throat-clearing, then asked, as if she felt she should be asking something, 'What kind of things do you like to do, Elfie?'

Elfie couldn't think what to say. Riding on the tops of buses. Roaming the streets as it was getting dark and the street lights were being lit. Kicking a ball round the park. They might not be the kind of things Mrs Trelawney meant. She glanced for help at Pa, who had overheard the question and come back to join them.

'She likes books, don't you, Elfie?'

'You can read then, dear?'

'She reads well. She likes to play draughts and is starting to learn chess.'

'My friend Joe is teaching me chess.'

'That's nice that you have a friend.'

'I've got several. Florrie's one of my best friends. She's the barmaid at the *Pig*.'

'I see.' Mrs Trelawney looked startled.

'Joe comes from the same place as Mr Trelawney's grandma.'

'The West Indies,' said Pa.

'Oh, yes, yes indeed.'

Funny, thought Elfie, she didn't seem to like that being brought up.

'Joe's black,' said Elfie.

'Black?'

'You know, his skin.' Elfie rubbed the back of her hand.

Rosalind giggled again. She needed a good slap, thought Elfie.

'Papa,' Rosalind called over to him, 'Elfie lives in a pig with a black boy.' She started up her silly giggling again.

Her father came to join them. 'You and I must have a game of chess, Elfie. Next time you come.'

Next time! Would there be a next time? Mrs Trelawney might say once was enough. More than enough.

Tea arrived. They had small triangular sandwiches, with fillings of cucumber, egg and cress, and boiled ham, with the crusts cut off, which amazed Elfie, for Ma always insisted they ate every bit of them. Nothing was to be wasted. As well as sandwiches there were cakes set daintily out on paper lace doilies on a three-tiered silver cake stand.

It was easier when everyone was eating and drinking and things were being passed round. Elfie took great care not to grab, gobble or drop anything.

Afterwards, Rosalind asked 'Do you want to see my bedroom?'

'What a capital idea, Rosalind!' said her father.

'Come on,' urged Rosalind.

'I bet she's bossy,' thought Elfie as she followed her. 'Used to getting her own way. Well, she ain't goin' to boss me around.'

Rosalind's bedroom had pale-pink walls and a deep-blue ceiling with silver stars. A dolls' house and dolls were sitting on the floor and Elfie felt a moment's panic as the room of the dead Arabella came back to her. If there had ever *been* an Arabella. Dowdy had told them they were still trying to find out.

'Nanny sleeps in here.' Rosalind opened a door to reveal a room opening off hers. It was half the size, painted cream, with plain, unvarnished furniture. 'It's her day off. All the servants have Sunday off, except for Swain, the coachman, and Ethel, who have Mondays. Papa says everyone needs a day off a week.'

'What other servants have you got?'

'There's Cook and Mrs Munn, the housekeeper, whom Mama calls her treasure, and Henry, the butler. That's all. How many do you have?'

'None.'

'None at all? But you must have *some*.'

'We do the work, us children. We wash the dishes and do the ironing and make the beds and take the washing to the laundry.'

That silenced Rosalind. She couldn't seem to

comprehend it.

Elfie had a look at the books on the shelves and took down *A Child's Garden of Verses*. Pa Bigsby had read it to them. It was by the same man who wrote *Treasure Island*, Robert Louis Stevenson. Pa had told them he was a Scotsman, which had interested Elfie, with her mother having been Scottish, and her grandparents. She'd started to think about them. Before they'd not seemed like real people. Pa said that when she was older she could go and find the place in Fife they'd come from.

'Do you want to read to me?' asked Rosalind.

'If you like.'

Elfie read aloud the poem *The Land of Counterpane*, about a boy who had to spend a lot of time in bed because he was ill. She was pleased with herself that she was able to read to Rosalind.

After that they played *Snakes and Ladders* and then it was time to go. Alfred Trelawney came in to say that Mr Bigsby was waiting for Elfie.

'You seem to be getting on well, the two of you?' He sounded pleased.

Rosalind slid her hand into her father's as they went downstairs, giving Elfie a little look that said, 'He's *my* papa.'

A final treat awaited Elfie: a ride home in the Trelawneys' private carriage!

When they arrived back at the *Pig and Whistle* Elfie asked Mr Swain, the coachman, to pump the horn to let everyone know they were back. The children came rushing out to examine the carriage and take turns at squeezing the horn, and the little ones clambered inside and didn't want to get out. Mr Swain didn't mind in the least. He let them play for a few minutes while he went into the *Pig and Whistle* and was rewarded with a pint of stout from Ma. Alcohol was not permitted to be sold on Sundays but she didn't sell him the stout, she gave it to him, and the door was shut so that nobody passing could see into the bar.

Everyone admired the Trelawney carriage, except for Ivy, of course, but Elfie expected that. She said the seats looked hard and the horse was scabby.

'You're a liar,' snapped Elfie.

'That'll do now, girls,' said Pa.

The next visit to the house on Hampstead Heath was easier. Both Elfie and Mrs Trelawney were less nervous. Mrs Trelawney stayed in the drawing room with Pa Bigsby while her husband took the children out on the heath to fly kites, which Elfie found great fun once she'd got the hang of it. Until she did, her string was in a continual tangle.

Rosalind grew tired of kite-flying and went home. Elfie and Alfred Trelawney stayed out to walk a little across the heath. She was still finding it difficult to think of him as her *father*.

'It's too fine a day to go inside,' he said.

'I like being outside,' she said.

'So do I!' He smiled at her, then sobered. 'Mr Bigsby has told me about your early life, Elfie.'

She hoped he hadn't said too much!

'You had a rotten time and I'm really sorry about that.'

'Not your fault. You didn't know about me.'

'If only I hadn't gone to Canada! I didn't want to go. I wanted to stay and marry your mother.'

'Why didn't you?'

'I was young, only twenty-one. My father said if I spent two years in Canada and still didn't want to go into the timber business at the end of it I could give it up. Which I did.'

He was sad now and so was she. They walked on in silence. She was thinking how it might have been if he had married her mum.

Eventually he spoke again. 'But I am very pleased to have found you now, Elfie.'

His eyes lit up. 'Come on, I've got something to show you!'

He led her back to the house and round to the coach house. He told her to cover her eyes and then he flung open the coach-house door, saying that she could look now!

Standing there was a brand-new black motor car!

'It's a French car, made by a firm called Renault. I went over to Paris myself to buy it.'

'It's lovely.'

'I'm going to drive you and Mr Bigsby home in it. It's

only meant for two so it'll be a bit of a squash but we'll manage.'

Elfie had never ridden in a motor car before. She didn't know anyone who had. Not even Pa Bigsby. Nor had she ever flown a kite before. Or had tea out of a silver teapot. Or sandwiches with their crusts cut off. She was doing so many new things that her head reeled by the time she went to bed at night.

Also, she had a father. That was new too.

'Well, this is going to be exciting,' said Pa Bigsby as he contemplated the car.

Alfred Trelawney helped him up into the seat and Elfie clambered up beside him, making herself as small as possible in order to leave room for the driver. He was putting on a pair of long leather gloves and goggles.

Then he cranked up the car until the engine spluttered into life and sprang on board to join them.

'Quite amazing,' said Pa Bigsby, shaking his head.

Elfie's father took hold of the steering wheel.

'Hang on to your hat, Mr Bigsby!' he cried and they were off.

Heads turned to watch them pass. Pa Bigsby rewarded some of them with a wave of his white-gloved hand. The breeze blew Elfie's hair about and she laughed. The car was open, unlike the carriage, which had a roof to keep out wind and rain.

Their arrival at the *Pig and Whistle* in a motor car made an even bigger stir than when they had come back in the carriage. At Elfie's request, Alfred Trelawney blew the horn, not once, but twice. The children came flooding out onto the pavement. This time, however, they were not allowed to climb inside the vehicle. They had to admire it from the pavement. Elfie told the little ones not to touch as they might leave smears on the paintwork.

Ma Bigsby came out, with Cuddles in her arms, to have a look too. She asked Mr Trelawney if he would care to come in and take some refreshment.

'Thank you, but another time perhaps? I must return home.'

'You'd be welcome any time, I'm sure.'

Elfie saw that he was looking at Joe. People always looked at him. He stood out, of course, because of the colour of his skin. He said it didn't bother him, he'd got used to it a long time ago. Well, he'd been that way since he'd been born, hadn't he?

'This is my friend Joe,' said Elfie.

'Pleased to meet you, Joe!' Alfred Trelawney stretched out his hand and Joe took it. 'Would you like to have a look at the engine?'

'I would, sir! I expect Billy would too.'

Alfred Trelawney opened up the engine and showed it to the boys. Billy had his nose inside straightaway. He loved machines.

When they'd finished their inspection and Alfred Trelawney was pulling on his big leather driving gloves, he turned to Joe. 'I hear you'd like to be a lawyer?'

Joe shrugged. 'Depends.'

'If you're interested, come into my chambers one day and we'll have a talk.'

At the third visit to Hampstead, Elfie was invited to stay the night. Rosalind asked if she could.

They had gone boating on the Thames followed by tea at a riverside cafe.

Pa Bigsby had not gone on the boat but had waited on the bank enjoying the spring sunshine. He said he was not a great lover of water, he preferred having his feet on dry land.

'What do you say, Elfie?' asked Alfred Trelawney. 'Would you like to stay the night?'

'Say yes!' commanded Rosalind.

'I haven't got my nightie with me.'

'We can easily sort that,' said Mrs Trelawney. 'You can borrow one of mine, it won't matter if it's too long.'

'Would you like to, Elfie?' asked Pa Bigsby.

'I think so.' She was not totally sure but felt she should give it a go.

Mr Swain took Pa home to the *Pig and Whistle* and Elfie stayed in Hampstead.

She was given one of the guest bedrooms, decorated in green and pink. A green silk eiderdown covered the bed, and green and pink damask curtains hung at the windows. She slept in a pale-green silk nightgown and when she awoke in the morning she could not remember where she was. She sat up and stared around her. Everything was in the room was beautiful. It was a lady's room.

They had breakfast in what they called 'the morning room', served by Ethel. The man of the house ate a large meal of kippers and bacon and scrambled eggs. Elfie, along with Rosalind, had fruit and porridge and a boiled egg with toast. And afterwards, they didn't have to wash the dishes. They didn't even have to clear the table. Elfie started to but Mrs Trelawney laid a hand on her arm and said it was not necessary.

'It's Ethel's job,' said Rosalind.

Alfred Trelawney drove Elfie home on his way to work. Before he cranked up the engine, he said, 'You know, Elfie, you might start to call me Father or Papa one of these days. But only if you wish of course.'

He did not wait for an answer. The engine was fired up and they were ready to go. They went roaring off down the drive into the road.

Chapter Twenty-Four: Alfred Trelawney Visits the Pig and Makes a Proposal

Alfred Trelawney sent a messenger with a note saying that he would like to call on them at the *Pig and Whistle*. He suggested an afternoon and asked if 4 pm would be convenient? Pa Bigsby wrote a note for the man to take back saying they would be delighted to receive Mr Trelawney.

Ma Bigsby and Elfie worked hard at shining up the parlour. Smudgy fingerprints were to be found all round the room if you looked for them. Only to be expected with small children about, said Ma. She busied herself with the furniture polish while Elfie worked on the brasses.

'I expect the Trelawneys' house is spit-clean?' said Ma.

'There's not a speck of dust to be seen anywhere,' Elfie assured her. 'The lavatory don't smell neither.'

'We'd better clean that and all. In case Mr Trelawney would ask to use it.'

Elfie thought he probably would not but agreed it was better to make sure. Ma was fussy, but their lavatory was used by an awful lot more people than the one on Hampstead Heath. In fact, the Trelawneys had two for themselves, and another for the servants. Rosalind had shown them to her.

Ma had baked a sponge cake in the morning and Mabel was now in the kitchen putting strawberry jam and clotted cream in the middle. Elfie wished they had a silver teapot and a three-tiered silver cake stand but Pa said he was certain that the absence of such items would not disturb Mr Trelawney. He himself had grown up in a big house with silver teapots and he was quite happy with their big brown kitchen pot. They did not intend to use that, however. Ma had unearthed from a cupboard a white teapot decorated with red roses that she had stowed away years ago, it being of no use in a household of thirteen. She had also found a china tea set that she and Pa had been given as a wedding present and had never used.

Their visitor arrived in the motor car at one minute to four and parked outside the *Pig and Whistle*'s front door. Ma had arranged for Joe and Billy to stand guard on it while he was inside.

'I'm not saying as anything would happen to it, Mr Trelawney, but better safe than sorry is my motto. A few ruffians with sticky fingers do hang about in these parts.'

'Everywhere in London, I fear.'

'Not so much where he lives,' thought Elfie. She'd not seen any sign of gangs lurking about the heath.

Joe and Billy were happy to look after the car. During the hour that the guest was inside they attracted an audience, amongst whom were Sad Sid and his friend Frankie and several other *Pig and Whistle* regulars, including Dowdy. With him around, the car was as safe as houses, said Ma.

Florrie had come in early for the special occasion and, at Elfie's request, was wearing her best pink satin blouse with the leg-of-mutton sleeves, her three-string pearl choker and extra-long dangling pearl earrings.

Mr Trelawney shook hands with her and everyone else and admired everything in the *Pig and Whistle*. He commented especially on the brasses.

'Elfie did them,' said Ma.

'My goodness! You must have worked hard, Elfie.'

'She can work hard when she puts her mind to it.'

'This is a present for the children from my wife.' Mr Trelawney handed Ma a large box of chocolates, tied up with purple satin ribbon.

'They will be much appreciated, thank you,' said Ma.

'Please convey our thanks and kind regards to Mrs Trelawney,' added Pa. 'And, pray, let us go up to the parlour where we may be more private.'

The visitor was given the best seat as was right. It was the only one which had its springs intact and didn't creak. Elfie had tried them all out earlier. The younger children liked to bounce from chair to chair when Ma was out of the room.

They had tea, Alfred Trelawney, Ma and Pa Bigsby and Elfie. Mabel had dusted the top of the sponge cake with icing sugar to make it look pretty. Their visitor ate a piece and pronounced it excellent, though he declined a second, saying that he had eaten heartily at luncheon. He did accept another cup of tea.

Afterwards, he wiped his hands on the linen napkin that had been carefully ironed by Mabel and sat back. Then he said, 'I have a proposal to make.'

They waited.

'It is really for you, Elfie.' He looked directly at her. 'You are my daughter and I would like to be your legal guardian and have you come and live with us.'

'In your house?'

'Yes, in our house.'

'What about Mrs Trelawney?'

'She would like it too. And Rosalind would love to have you as her elder sister. She has become very attached to you, I'm sure you must realize that?'

Elfie said nothing. She didn't know what to say. Leave the *Pig* and go and live in Trelawneys' big house in faraway Hampstead? If her head had been reeling before, it was in a spin now. Pa had once told her that when you didn't know what to say, say nothing until you do know. She was inclined to let things come spilling straight out, and often they were rubbish, she knew that.

'I would like to do it for your dear mother's sake but also for my own,' Alfred Trelawney went on. 'For I too have become very attached to you, Elfie.'

She couldn't have got any words out then if she'd tried. She had a big lump in her throat again.

'I would enrol you in a good private girl's school in Hampstead. And on Saturday mornings you could attend the dancing academy with Rosalind.'

Elfie wondered what kind of dancing they would do at a place like that. Florrie had been trying to teach her the polka. So far she hadn't been doing very well. She usually tramped on Florrie's feet and they ended up in a heap, laughing.

'And you would be able to come back and visit your friends here, of course.'

All eyes were on her.

'This is a very big decision for Elfie,' said Pa gravely.

'I am well aware of that,' said Alfred Trelawney. 'You must take plenty of time to think, Elfie. I would not want to rush you. But it would make me a very happy man if you were to accept.'

Chapter Twenty-Five:
Elfie Decides

'It would be a wonderful opportunity for you, Elfie,' said Pa Bigsby. 'One that would be difficult to pass up.'

'Its not often that any of our orphans get such an offer,' added Ma.

'I can recall only two or three occasions when a parent has turned up to claim their son or daughter,' said Pa.

'But they were never toffs like Mr Trelawney, were they, Pa?' said Ma.

'No, indeed. Your father is obviously a man of considerable means, Elfie. He confided to me that his wife herself is wealthy.'

'You'd never lack for nothing.' Ma nodded approvingly.

'Not that money is everything,' cautioned Pa.

'It helps though,' put in Ma. 'And Mr Trelawney is a very nice gent.'

'Extremely nice,' agreed Pa.

'Her too?' asked Ma.

'Mrs Trelawney also seems very pleasant. Her husband tells me that she is a good and kind woman.'

'Dutiful, I'd imagine?'

'Mr Trelawney assured me of that.'

'And you'd have a little sister, Elfie,' said Ma.

'She's spoilt rotten,' said Elfie, finding her tongue.

'I'm sure you could soon sort that out!' said Ma.

'You must think it over, Elfie,' advised Pa.

Elfie still couldn't think.

She went to look for Florrie.

Florrie said, 'Aren't you the lucky girl? Imagine, a beautiful big bedroom all to yourself! Lovely clothes. Anything you want!'

Billy said, 'Cor, ain't you the lucky duck? You'll get drove about in his motor car! Will you ask 'im to give us a turn in it?'

Everybody had something to say.

'Don't go, Elfie,' pleaded Nancy, clinging on to her hand.

'We don't want you to go,' said Dora. 'We won't have no one to tell us scary stories.'

Elfie had taken to telling them ghost stories in bed, mostly about a pig that haunted the house playing his whistle.

Ivy didn't say anything to her but Elfie overheard her talking in a loud voice to Mabel. 'I 'ope she goes! It'll be good riddance!'

Mabel said, 'I'm sorry you're going, Elfie, but I'm

pleased for you.' She sounded wistful, as if she would have liked to have had the chance herself.

'I ain't decided yet,' said Elfie.

'But you wouldn't turn it down, would you?' Mabel couldn't believe it.

Cuddles wasn't saying anything but he sucked his thumb extra hard and stared at Elfie as if he knew something was up.

Dowdy said, when he dropped in, 'You'd be daft not to go. It's the opportunity of a lifetime. Half the kids in London would give their right arm for the chance.'

Sad Sid said in his most mournful voice, 'I 'ear you're leavin' us?'

'I ain't decided yet,' said Elfie.

She had a headache.

Joe was the only one who wasn't saying anything.

Elfie was glad when Florrie and Dowdy came back from their Sunday outing to announce that they were engaged to be married. She was pleased that they'd got round to it but also because it gave everyone something else to talk about.

Florrie came in holding out her left hand to show off the little sparkling ring on her fourth finger. Nobody asked if it was a real diamond. Florrie's eyes were sparkling too.

'This calls for champagne!' cried Ma.

She popped the cork which flew up and hit the ceiling.

Pa called for three cheers. 'Here's health and happiness to Florrie and Kieron!' He raised his glass.

'Florrie and Kieron,' repeated Ma.

'Florrie and Dowdy,' chanted the children.

'Hip, hip!' cried Pa three times in a row.

Dowdy was blushing, Florrie laughing and making her earrings swing.

Elfie sidled up to her. 'Can I be your bridesmaid?'

'Oh, all right!' Florrie smiled at her. 'But I'm going to have Mabel and Ivy too. And the twins can be flower girls.'

'Not *Ivy*!'

'I can't leave her out.'

'But I 'ate her and she 'ates me.'

'*Hate*, Elfie! Pa'd be mad if he heard you.'

He had heard her. Later, when the excitement had died down, he asked Elfie to come up to his study.

'I know you don't like Ivy,' he began.

'I don't. I can't help it.'

'Yes, you can. I want to tell you something about her. She had a really bad time before she came here.'

Elfie tried to interrupt again but he held up his hand. 'Oh, I know you did too. All our orphans did. But Ivy's not an orphan.'

'What's she doing here then?'

'She's got a mum and dad somewhere but they don't want her.'

'Don't blame them,' muttered Elfie.

'Now, Elfie!' Pa was unusually stern.

Elfie hung her head, just a little.

Pa continued, 'When Ivy lived with them they beat her and starved her and then one day they just dumped her out in the street. She was black and blue from bruises. It makes it worse in a way, don't you see? I mean, you know your mum didn't dump you. Nor your dad either.'

Elfie was quiet. She could see what he meant even if she didn't want to.

'You might not come to be best friends with Ivy but perhaps you could try to stop hating her.'

She certainly couldn't imagine being best friends! Pa was waiting for an answer. 'She'd have to stop hating me too.'

'I shall talk to her also.'

'She wants me to go.'

'That must not influence your decision.'

'Do you want me to?'

'Of course not, Elfie. But what Ma and I want has nothing to do with it. It is your life and we want what is best for you.'

Pa did not ask her if she had made up her mind. Thank goodness for that! She was sick of people asking. Even the shopkeepers kept at it. They were all agog at the idea of her going to live on Hampstead Heath. 'You'll be the little Lady Muck then. You won't have time for the likes of us.'

Her head was in a constant whirl. One minute she'd think of the wonderful time she would have living in a lovely house with her father, her *pa*, how she would wear beautiful clothes and not have to wash any more dishes or iron sheets and pillow cases, or take the washing to the horrible old steam laundry, or have to try to like Ivy, and the next she'd think that she couldn't bear to leave the *Pig* and Ma and Pa Bigsby and Florrie and the twins and Mabel and Vicky and Albert and Sam and Cuddles. And Joe.

She decided to go and talk to Joe when he came back. He'd gone to visit her father, Alfred Trelawney, solicitor-at-law, in his chambers in Covent Garden.

She hung about in the street until she saw him coming.

They walked up to the park. She could go there now without thinking about the Do-Goods or, at least, not to let the thought of them trouble her overly much. They were still awaiting trial and when it came up she'd have to give evidence. Pa Bigsby had told her not to worry about that as he and Dowdy would accompany her, as would Mr Trelawney. He had been very upset when he'd heard about that episode. The police hadn't been able to find any trace of Arabella and were coming to the conclusion that she had never existed.

It was a warm, sunny day. The trees were thick with leaves and the flowers in full bloom.

'So how did you get on?' asked Elfie.

'Great. Your dad's a fine man, Elfie.' Joe couldn't stop smiling. 'And you'll never guess?'

'What?'

'He's offered to give me a job in his office next year when I'm fourteen. Just odd jobs to start with but he says that if I show promise as I get older it may be possible for me to train as a lawyer.'

'I'm so pleased, Joe!'

'He's interested in trying to do something to help street kids. He says he'd never thought much about them before until Pa told him your story.'

She wished Pa hadn't told him the whole story. Some of it hadn't been very nice.

She sighed. 'Joe, I don't know what to do. If it was you, and your dad came back, would you go and live with him?'

Joe did not hesitate. 'Of course I would. I loved my dad.'

Joe's answer had only made it worse.

It wasn't that Elfie didn't love her father. When she thought about it she realized that she did. It might not be quite the way Joe felt, for he'd known his dad a lot longer, and from the moment he was born. She had only known hers for weeks. But she felt he was *like* her, even though he might seem so different. He got excited about boating on the river or flying kites and he'd do something on the spur of the moment. Like when he'd hugged her that first time they met in his chambers. Mrs Trelawney held back more. Elfie liked her well enough, however.

The trouble was that she loved Ma and Pa Bigsby more and she liked having lessons in Pa's school and hated the idea of going to a fancy girls' school where they might make fun of her if she forgot, and dropped her aitches. She went back to talk to Pa.

He said, 'You shouldn't let that stop you or you'll never get on in life. You would settle into a new school and make new friends, given time, the way you did here. Remember how you felt when you first came to the *Pig*?'

Elfie went back to thinking. Her dad – she was starting to think of him as that more and more – was coming the following day to get her answer.

Elfie, her dad and Ma and Pa Bigsby retreated to the study and closed the door. In the parlour on the floor below the orphans were unusually quiet. Joe was trying to read but finding it difficult to concentrate. He kept looking up. There were no sounds coming from overhead, no clue as to what was going on.

At last, they heard the door open, followed by an exchange of voices and then the tread of feet on the stairs. Joe went to the window and looked down on the street where the Trelawney carriage was waiting. Mr Swain was sitting on the box, holding the horse's reins loosely.

Alfred Trelawney emerged on to the pavement with Elfie and Pa Bigsby. He shook hands with Pa and embraced Elfie, holding on to her for a moment, then he climbed into the carriage, the coachman cracked his whip and the horse trotted off. Alfred Trelawney waved from the carriage window.

Seconds later, the parlour door flew open, and in came Elfie. She was wearing her red velvet dress that she'd put on especially for her father's visit. The lace collar was askew and her new white stockings were twisted. Ma Bigsby had bought them just the day before, after she'd taken a look through Elfie's drawer and thrown out a heap of stuff. She said she had never known a girl as rough on her clothes as Elfie.

Elfie paused. She was out of breath, as if she'd run pell-mell up the stairs.

'What you goin' to do then?' asked Mabel, breaking the silence.

'I'm staying at the *Pig*,' announced Elfie.

The twins cheered.

'Honestly?' said Joe. 'You're really going to stay?'

'Cross my heart.'

'Ain't you goin' to see your dad again?' asked Billy.

He sounded horrified. He was probably thinking about the motor car.

'Course. I'm going to visit him at weekends and stay Sunday night. He wanted me to stay Saturday nights too but I told him I didn't want to miss Saturday night at the *Pig*.'

Joe began to laugh.

'Well, it's the best night of the week, ain't it?' Elfie demanded.

'*Isn't* it.' Joe laughed again.

'You wouldn't want to miss it, would you?'

'No, I wouldn't.'

Elfie didn't want to miss all the fuss leading up to Florrie's wedding either. Or the treat to Southend-on-Sea that Pa was organising. It promised to be the best outing that they'd ever had at the *Pig and Whistle*.

Her father was going to give Ma and Pa money to cover her keep with extra to buy treats for everybody. She didn't say anything about that now. They'd find out later. And he'd promised to give Joe and Billy a ride in his motor car.

There was another thing that Elfie didn't want to miss. Having Joe to play chess with, and talk to, about all sorts of things. But she wasn't going to tell him that.

'I'm glad you're staying,' he said.

'We all are,' said Pa, who had come in with Ma and Florrie behind Elfie.

'Even though you drive us all up the pole at times,' said Ma, who was also wearing her Sunday dress, and smiling.

'Who, me?' said Elfie, doing her best to look innocent.

'Yes, you!' said Pa Bigsby.

Also by Joan Lingard published by Catnip

The File on Fraulein Berg

It's hard to spot the enemy within.

1944. Belfast. The war drags on. Kate, Harriet and Sally read spy stories and imagine themselves dropping over enemy lines to perform deeds of great daring.

When Fraulein Berg, a real German, arrives at their school it doesn't take them long to work out that their new teacher is a spy. Now the girls have a mission. To watch her. Follow her. Track down every secret. Prove she is the enemy.

But the File on Fraulein Berg reveals a very different story – one that will haunt Kate for the rest of her life.

A classic story from the award-winning author of the *Kevin and Sadie* novels.